I0608435

WDM PRESENTS: SHORT FICTION FROM 2019

DEB LOGAN

DEBBIE MUMFORD

WDM
Publishing

COPYRIGHT

INTRODUCTION

2019 was great a year for WDM Publishing. We published several novels and collections as well as the short fiction included in this volume.

When they weren't writing novels, our authors produced short fantasy and science fiction tales, and even one historical piece.

This volume opens with a moving LitRPG story, moves into the far reaches of space, and then explores a quiet apocalypse before returning to the contemporary world. We end the volume with a Deb Logan urban fantasy, followed by a short historical fiction tale by Debbie Mumford.

We hope you enjoy 2019's short fiction.

EMMA: A FEYLAND DRYAD

1

I held my breath as Uncle Jim lowered the helmet onto my head and adjusted the interface to the grav chair he'd designed specifically for me. He maintained a steady stream of explanations as he worked, while I fought to focus on his words, to stay grounded in reality, to not allow my hopes to soar too high. If the interface didn't perform as he expected, I didn't want to fall too far. I released my breath and concentrated on what he was actually saying ... not what I desperately wanted to hear.

"All right, Emma," he said, hands dropping to his sides. "I want you to relax. When you're ready to begin, think very clearly *Enter Feyland*. When you want to quit, think *Leave Feyland*. Do you understand?"

I blinked twice. My version of yes, and prayed that this new brainchild of Uncle Jim's would work. I tried to relax. It should work. Why wouldn't it? After all, my uncle was the famous James Carter, chief designer of the hottest full-D immersive game on the market.

"Good. I'm switching the interface on ... now."

Uncle Jim looked almost as nervous as I felt. His light brown hair was a mess—he kept running his fingers through it and tugging the longer bits on top until they stood nearly straight—and his thick glasses sat slightly askew on the bridge of his nose. Right now he'd make a great mad scientist in a sci-fi vid. A wave of fondness washed over me. He'd always been kind to me, had worked to understand me, and now I watched as he turned the dial that could change my life forever.

He smiled. "Now it's all up to you, Emma."

I closed my eyes, held my hopes and fears tight, and thought, *Enter Feyland.* A black shield slid into place over my eyes, isolating me from the sunny conservatory where I spent my days. A large gold *F* outlined in flames appeared and hauntingly lovely music filled the air. Golden words replaced the *F* and my adventure began.

WELCOME TO FEYLAND
A VirtuMax Production

A welcome screen replaced the title and as the screen changed, the words morphed from gold to scarlet before turning to ash and seeming to blow away. This was better than watching vids with my dad. This was all-encompassing. I was there. I could almost feel the breeze and smell the ash. The game hadn't even started and already it rocked!

As Uncle Jim had explained, my first task was to create a character. After reading through the list of classes, I chose a dryad. My sense of humor might be warped, but I found a certain poetic fitness in playing a character whose main defense would be to turn into a tree and become immobile.

Trumpets blared and the screen flared with golden light. Dizzying disorientation seized me and my stomach lurched as if my chair had suddenly dropped several feet. I closed my eyes and willed myself to calmness. I was no stranger to unpleasant surprises. I could handle this.

Taking a deep breath, I opened my eyes.

I was standing in a woodland clearing, surrounded by white-barked trees. Shock froze me in place, my reality shattered by those three words: *I was standing!*

Not sitting. Not reclining. Not supported by anyone or anything. I was standing in a clearing, on my own two feet, as if it were the most natural thing in the world. As if I were the normal girl I'd always dreamed of being. As if I'd just awakened from a hideous nightmare to find myself here, in this peaceful wooded glade, surrounded by white-barked trees with silvery leaves, under a clear blue sky, with soft moss beneath my leather-booted feet and encircled by a ring of mushrooms.

Laughter bubbled up inside. I wanted to jump for joy! I'd read that phrase a thousand times, but never expected to feel the impulse. Could I actually do it? Could I step over those mushrooms? Their jaunty red caps sprinkled with white spots encouraged me to try.

"Go ahead," they seemed to say. "You can do it. You can do anything. This is Feyland!"

Gathering my courage, I did what all the doctors had said I'd never do. I took a step, and after that, another, and suddenly I was running and jumping and twirling and waving my arms with abandon. I was alive! My body was fully functional!

I laughed and cried and danced and celebrated the enormous gift Uncle Jim had given me. The blessed man had no idea what I felt. How could he? How could anyone whose body behaved the way it was supposed to understand how I felt?

Exhausted by joy, I flopped onto the mossy greenness and rolled, unconcerned about staining my comfortable brown tunic and deep green tights. I closed my eyes and breathed in the goodness of the glade. A cool breeze kissed my face and ruffled my short dark hair. The air smelled of growing things. Rich dark soil, fragrant flowers, and mossy grass bruised by my frantic exertions.

What a perfect day!

As my heart rate settled, I heard a movement. Booted feet on soft earth? Opening my eyes, I sat up and glanced around. A young man, boy really, probably a teen like myself, leaned against one of the white-barked trees at the edge of the clearing.

He was dressed in a loose linen shirt with a dark brown vest laced across his chest and matching brown pants. His hair was golden brown and when he smiled at me, it was like the sun emerging from behind a cloud.

"Hello," he said. "You're new here, aren't you?"

I nodded and scrambled to my feet (to my feet! All by myself!), brushing leaves and grass from my clothing and trying to contain the giddy laughter that still wanted to bubble over.

"I've been watching you," he said, and I swear his eyes actually twinkled. "You seem happy to be here."

"I am," I answered. "This is amazing. I never want to *Leave Feyland*."

And just like that, my adventure ended. The shield retracted and I found myself blinking at Dad and Uncle Jim. Back in the real world ... where I was so terribly afflicted with spastic quadriplegia that I couldn't speak or even sit in a grav chair without straps to hold my body erect.

2

_I_ wanted to scream, to rage at the injustice of that simple phrase pulling me back to a reality I didn't want to acknowledge.

Uncle Jim must have recognized the anger and disappointment on my face. He knelt before my grav chair, and placing his hands on mine where they were strapped in place said, "It's okay, Emma. I can see you have something to say. Let's try the interface's other function."

I frowned. The interface had another function? Something other than allowing me to play the full-D game that Uncle Jim and his company had developed?

"I know it's hard," Uncle Jim continued, "but I want you to relax. Be calm."

When my breathing regulated and my face relaxed as much as it ever did, he nodded.

"Good girl. Now, compose your thoughts. When you're ready, think _Activate Speech Mode_, then think what you'd like to say. When you want your thoughts to be private again, think _Deactivate_. Understand?"

I blinked twice.

He grinned and held crossed fingers up where I could see them. "Good luck!"

I closed my eyes, thought about all the things I wanted to say. All the things I'd waited my entire life to express, but not now. Now I just needed to tell Dad and Uncle Jim about the interface ... and the magic of Feyland.

Concentrating with my whole being, I thought, *Activate Speech Mode*, and then, *Does this work?*

An oddly mechanical female voice shouted the words.

Dad stumbled forward and dropped to his knees in front of my grav chair. His fingers trembled as he stroked my cheek. "I hear you, baby. I hear you!" Tears brimmed in his eyes and he turned to Uncle Jim. "Thank you, Jim. I can't ..."

Uncle Jim put a hand on Dad's shoulder. "There's no need, Kent. I'm just so pleased it's working."

They both looked at me.

I'd have grinned if I could. Instead I thought, *Feyland is amazing, Uncle Jim! Dad, you wouldn't believe it. Everything works there. My body works! I can stand and walk and run ... and I can talk. It's ... it's like a dream come true!*

The voice, my pseudo-voice, had a mechanical twang, but the volume regulated now that I knew it worked and wasn't pushing the thoughts with quite that initial intensity. The voice also sped up and increased in pitch in response to my emotions ... and it was nearly instantaneous. A real-time echo of my thoughts. I deactivated it so I could think while I waited for their response.

Uncle Jim beamed. "Emma, that's wonderful." He paused, a little frown creasing his brow. "But why did you come back so soon if everything functioned correctly? Jennet can spend hours in that game."

Jennet. Uncle Jim's daughter. My cousin. The girl who was everything I should've been if life had been kinder. Even though she was only two years older than me, the differences between us were huge. Jennet was perfect, while my difficult and traumatic birth left me with a severe form of Cerebral Palsy. We should've been best buds. We'd grown up together. Our mothers had been sisters and for most of our lives we'd lived only a few miles apart ... but it's hard to get to know someone when you can't communicate. Now though ... maybe we could become real friends at last. Even beyond family ties, we had a lot in common. We'd both lost our mothers a few years ago. We were both motherless girls with overworked, overburdened fathers. Too bad Uncle Jim's work with VirtuMax had caused them to move to Crestview a while back.

But I could think about my family issues later. Right now, I had more pressing matters to discuss. A chill ran through me. I never imagined the word *discuss* would apply to me!

I activated my speech mode and explained what had happened. "Could you please change the exit phrase, Uncle Jim? I was having a great time, and I'd just met another player. We were talking when I said, 'I never want to leave Feyland,' and suddenly the game ended and the interface brought me back here."

Uncle Jim's face cleared and he laughed aloud. "Of course! I can fix that right now. What would you like it to be? Obviously it needs to be something you can remember easily, but not something that you're likely to say in casual conversation." He grinned and straightened his glasses. "I evidently failed on that last bit."

Dad changed position so he was sitting on the floor by my grav chair instead of kneeling. "I can't believe I can hear you, Emma. After all this time, you can actually tell us what you want." He leaned back on his hands, a thoughtful expression on his face.

"What about *Deactivate Feyland*?" Uncle Jim asked. "That way both of your 'stop program' thoughts will be similar."

Dad nodded. "I like that. What do you think, Emma?"

I wished I could nod, too. Of course, I wished I could do a thousand things that my body was incapable of. Right now, I needed to focus on the amazing gift I'd been given. "I can remember that, and I can't imagine that phrase coming up in conversation."

Uncle Jim stepped to the laptop computer that he'd connected to the interface and began typing. "I'll fix that right now, Emma, and then I'll leave you and your dad alone so you can talk." He glanced up and smiled. "You can continue your game after you've had a chance to catch up."

"Thank you, Uncle Jim," I said, savoring my ability to speak. "For everything!"

3

___

*T*wo hours later, I reentered Feyland.

Once again I stood inside a ring of red-capped mushrooms with cheerful white spots, in a forest clearing surrounded by white-barked trees with silver leaves. The sun shone from high in the prettiest blue sky I had ever seen and a light breeze played with the ends of my hair. I hopped over the mushrooms, grinning, and twirled. Feyland might be an illusion, but it was one my mind welcomed. I was free! From my chair and the restrictions of my damaged body.

I glanced around the glade and spotted a path leading into the woods. Time to really begin the game. I picked up the oak staff that was part of my costume and fingered the tender twigs and budding leaves that adorned its crown. Magic was awesome. It gave me working arms and legs and let a staff that should be dead wood sprout greenery. How cool was this place?

I marched across the clearing to the mouth of the path, stepped onto its pebbled surface and called, "Watch out, Feyland. I'm a dryad and my name is Emma ... and I'm free at last!"

My heart beat with joy as I skipped down the path, living

staff in hand. I almost started singing—just because I could—but the birdsong and the breeze rustling through the leaves was too pretty to compete with.

I'd just settled down to a quick walk when the path widened into another clearing. Instead of a circle of mushrooms, this one held a low slung cottage of white-washed stone and a thatched roof. Window boxes of bright red flowers hung below each of the two windows. A Dutch door stood between them, with the upper portion open. A large oak tree stood beside and just behind the cottage, its wide canopy shading the small dwelling.

Stepping into the clearing, I stopped and leaned against my staff, enjoying the peace of the glade. What a charming place to live! I tried to imagine what kind of person lived in such an idyllic cottage. This was Feyland, so the inhabitant would undoubtedly be some race of faerie. Perhaps a dryad? The oak tree certainly seemed to be protecting the place. But I didn't think dryads lived in houses. An elf?

Before I could speculate further, a gnarled old man appeared at the door. His face was as wrinkled as a raisin, and nearly the same deep purple color. The top of his head was bald, but white hair streamed from a half circle that ran around his scalp from ear to ear. Bushy white eyebrows and a luxurious mustache that flowed into a full beard completed his hairy appearance.

He eyed me from head to toe then met my gaze. "Who are you and why are you disturbing the quiet of my glade?" he asked in a rather belligerent tone.

"I, uh, I'm a dryad," I said, not quite sure how to answer. "I'm just out for a walk and the path led me here."

"Just out for a walk, heh?" He looked me over again and scowled. "Well, if you want to cross my glade, you'll have to pay my fee. If not, you can just turn around and go back the way you came."

Hmm. This must be the first quest in the game. Since I didn't really want to return to my grav chair in the conservatory, I really had little choice.

"What is your fee, good sir?"

"There's a stream just beyond my oak tree. Bring me a fish for my supper and I'll give you a token that will allow you safe passage through the Forest of Fear."

The Forest of Fear? That sounded ominous. Safe passage would definitely be a good item to add to my inventory. I glanced at the massive tree. I hadn't seen any sign of a stream and I hadn't heard the gurgle of flowing water. Maybe it was a bug in the game, but a system so intricate that it could make a quadriplegic girl believe she was walking ought to be able to handle a little thing like the sound of running water. Was this funny looking little man lying to me?

And that wasn't even the main question. If I managed to find the stream, what would I do? I didn't have any idea how to catch a fish! I mean, I'd listened to enough audiobooks to know people used fishing poles, or rods and reels, but I didn't have any of that stuff. I looked at my staff. Could I use it for a fishing pole? Maybe, but what about a hook and a line? Could I catch one with my bare hands? I'd heard of folks who could, but I usually couldn't use my hands for anything, so I certainly didn't have any experience with such things.

Still, what did it matter? I'd come to Feyland to play a game, so play I would.

"I accept your offer, good sir." A soft chime sounded. Interesting. I hoped that was a good sign. "I'll return with your fish as soon as I can."

"See that you do," he said with a sniff, and disappeared into his home.

I walked past the cottage toward the spreading oak. With every step, the sound of water grew stronger. At first it was a barely detectable gurgle, but by the time I reached the tree, the stream fairly sang. My steps quickened. I could hardly wait to see it, for its melody sang of splashing rivulets, of currents crashing into rocks and then swirling past. It sang of joy and freedom, and my heart sang with it!

My feet skipped across the meadow between the oak and the stream, and I laughed with joy at my unfettered movement. I understood the water's song because my heart was singing the same one.

I ran along the bank until I came to a young willow over-hanging the stream. Once upon a time the current had cut into the bank just beside its roots and then swirled away. Now the willow shaded a deep, quiet pool. A good-sized rock guarded the stream bank, and I sat, trailing my fingers in the water. The movement created soft ripples in the cool, dark water, distorting my reflection.

As the ripples dissipated, another reflection appeared in the water. A golden haired youth. I turned to see the boy I'd met earlier standing a few feet behind me.

"You came back," he said, smiling. And just like earlier, that smile made the day seem brighter, like the sun had ratcheted up a few notches. "You left so suddenly, I wasn't sure you would."

My cheeks heated with a blush. "Yes," I said. "That was a mistake. A glitch in my interface. I didn't mean to disappear."

"I'm glad. Your words certainly didn't seem to match your actions!" He grinned, and then his expression sobered. "Will the *glitch* happen again?"

How odd. He almost stumbled over the word glitch. As if he'd never heard it before. As if he didn't understand what it meant.

"No. My uncle fixed the problem. I'm all set now." His expression cleared and he dropped to the grass beside my rock. "I'm new to Feyland," I continued, "but I don't recognize your costume. What class player are you?"

He glanced away, picked up a pebble and tossed it into the quiet water. The movement caught my attention and we both watched the ripples as they moved outward, only to be lost in the froth of current in the center of the stream.

"I'm a faerie knight," he said. "A member of the Bright Court."

I continued to watch the water as it splashed and swirled in the dappled sunlight. Joy personified.

"A faerie knight? I don't remember that being an option. Do you suppose we're playing different versions of the game?"

"No," he said quietly, his voice so low his words were almost drowned by the noise of the stream. "It is not an option for humans ... and I am not playing a game. At least, not the kind you imagine."

My heart pounded so hard my vision turned gray around the edges. I didn't understand. Something was wrong with what he'd just said. Should I leave? Should I think my safe words and flee the game?

Probably.

But he hadn't done anything to threaten me, and I wanted to understand. If I could.

I turned away from the sparkling water and studied him. Same golden brown hair. Same linen shirt with dark brown vest and pants. He was the same boy I'd met earlier. I hadn't felt threatened then, and I didn't now. Only his words were strange.

"I don't understand," I said, and he turned his attention back to me. Our gazes met and locked. His eyes fascinated me, green with interesting little flecks of orange. I could get lost studying those eyes, forget all about my questions and concerns. I closed my eyes and shook my head. When I opened them again, I concentrated on his hair instead, the way it waved across his forehead and curled around his ears.

Good lord! What was it with this guy? Even his hair was mesmerizing!

I licked my lips and dropped my gaze to my own hands. "What do you mean, 'it's not an option for humans'? You're human, aren't you?"

He gave a little bark of laughter and I glanced up again.

"No. I am not human, but you are safe with me, child of man. I knew what you were the moment I saw you. You think you are playing a game, but you have stumbled into my realm. The true Realm of Faerie."

My eyes widened and my pulse rate soared. "But...but...that's not possible! Faerie doesn't exist!"

His smile was a little sad now. "Oh, I assure you it is and it does. Others have stumbled across the threshold before you, little one. We, all of us who live in the realm, have standing orders to bring any humans we find before the Bright King."

"And the little raisin man who sent me to this stream? Does he have those orders too?"

My knight nodded. "He sent you here and alerted me." He paused, studying my face, his own creased with a frown. "But ... I cannot say why, but I find myself reluctant to take you to the king. There is something about you that is different from other humans who have wandered into Faerie. Something sad and joyous, innocent and ancient, all at the same time. You perplex me, little human." He stopped again and then asked, "Will you gift me with your name?"

Alarm bells rang in my brain. I'd heard lots of fairy tales. I'd lived vicariously through the quests and magical encounters recorded in books. I'd always believed them to be fiction, stories conjured from the imaginations of their writers, but now.... Now I didn't know what to think.

But one of the recurring themes in such fantasies is that names have power. And here was a self-professed faerie knight, a guy who claimed not to be human, asking me to trust him with my name, my essence.

"You first," I said, though how I expected to know if he told the truth, I'll never know.

"In your tongue, my name would be Brendan, but my true name is Bréanainn."

His name sounded something like "Bree-nin," but pronounced like the breeze whispering through the silver leaves of the white-barked trees.

"Thanks," I said, "but I think I'll stick with Brendan. My name is Emma." There. I'd told him the truth, but not all of it. He didn't need to know my full name.

He rose to his knees before the rock where I sat, took my hand, and bent to kiss it. "It is my very great honor to know you, Emma." Without releasing my hand, he raised his eyes and met my gaze. "Know this, if it is within my power to do so, I will protect you as you journey through Faerie."

My jaw dropped. If the old tales were true, faeries didn't lie. They might withhold information or they might lead you to jump to the wrong conclusion, but they didn't tell outright lies. If he really was a faerie, if this wasn't just another bit of programming in the game, Brendan had just pledged to protect me.

A giddiness to rival discovering that my body worked rose up and nearly swamped me. I smiled so broadly my cheeks hurt.

When my emotions were semi under control, I thanked him, at least, as much as I dared. That's another bit of fairy lore: faeries don't go in for thanks. "I don't really know what's going on, but I understand what you just said. I'm honored, Brendan."

He nodded and sat back, leaning on his palms. "I hope that someday you will explain the inconsistencies I sense in you," he said. "You fascinate me, Emma ... who pretends to be a dryad in a game that is not a game."

I laughed aloud, stood and spun around. I spent enough time sitting in my grav chair in the conservatory. I wanted to run and jump and dance while I had a body that could do all those things!

"Do I really have to catch a fish for the little raisin guy?" I asked.

Brendan grinned. "Not if you do not wish to, milady. And you should know, the *little raisin guy* is one of our best gatekeepers. He is a tomten who followed the Vikings from their lands to ours and finally found his way to Faerie. The Bright Court is now his home."

"So," I said, "the Bright Court takes in strangers and wanderers?" A thought so daring I wasn't sure I should allow it to take root pushed its way into my mind. Could I? Would I dare? Should I even wonder if it would be possible for me to become part of Brendan's Bright Court? It would mean leaving the human world behind, but that wouldn't be so bad. I mean, it wouldn't exactly be a loss to leave my grav chair and my hospital bed and my poor, damaged, quadriplegic body behind. But it would also mean leaving Dad ... and good people who cared about me, like Uncle Jim.

Besides, I didn't know enough about this place yet to even consider such a question. Better to file it away, somewhere deep and dark, where it wouldn't tempt me to ask. Right now, I should just enjoy the game and Brendan's friendship, and glory in the gift Uncle Jim had given me.

Brendan and I danced to the music of stream and birdsong, away from the water and back up into the meadow. We laughed and twirled and leapt and ran until we fell into an exhausted heap among the sweet green grass and fragrant wildflowers.

I was still catching my breath when Brendan jumped to standing and froze.

"What?" I asked, alarmed, but he waved me to silence as he scanned the horizon.

The next thing I knew, he'd pulled me to my feet. "Your game gives you specific powers, does it not?"

I nodded. "I have something called Wasp Sting and Thorn Bite," I said, "and I can turn into an oak for short periods of time."

"That should suffice," he said, still scanning the sky.

"Brendan, what's wrong?"

"The Wild Hunt is coming. Our friend the tomten must have alerted the court to your presence."

"What should I do?" I asked, fear making my voice shrill. "Should I leave?"

"That might be best."

I took a deep breath and reached for the calm I always held in reserve for hospital visits and painful tests. When I felt centered, I said, "Deactivate Feyland."

Nothing happened.

I didn't return to my grav chair in the conservatory. I was still in a grassy meadow sprinkled with wildflowers staring at Brendan.

He tipped his head and cocked an eyebrow at me. "Why do you remain?"

"It didn't work. What do I do now?" Even I could hear the sound of pounding hooves and pack dogs barking.

"They will arrive in mere moments. The Horned One's magic must have trapped you here. Quickly, become a tree."

Oh, wow! Just like that, do something I'd never tried before. I scolded myself for not having used all of my items at least once, so that I knew what they'd do.

No time for if-onlys. I had to act.

I checked my inventory, chose Be An Oak, and activated the item.

My arms and legs snapped together as my body became the trunk of a tree. My hair stood on end, the strands separating and lengthening, reaching for the sky and blossoming into a canopy of limbs, twigs and glossy green leaves. My toes stretched into the meadow's soil, lengthening and digging, becoming roots that held me firmly in place. My face melted into bark, and while I couldn't exactly see, I perceived all that happened around me.

I was immobile, locked inside a protective barrier of wood and leaf, unable to communicate with Brendan.

Entirely too much like the Emma I'd left behind in the real world.

Panic swamped me, but I fought through it. I'd lived this way my entire life. Only today had I truly been able to communicate in the real world and dance and play in Feyland. I could bear this. I knew this. And, most importantly, I knew this self-imposed immobility would end.

Just like I knew that my silence had ended at home.

Uncle Jim had given me a miracle. I still couldn't dance and play at home, but thanks to the interface, I'd never be a prisoner in my own skull again.

I could endure being a tree in Feyland, and I could endure spastic quadriplegia at home. The interface had freed me.

Brendan's voice filtered through my fevered thoughts. "They come. Do nothing until I say it is safe."

I rustled my leaves in acknowledgement.

Brendan sat at my base, leaning against my trunk. He whistled merrily and was soon surrounded by a pack of milling, snuffling dogs with evil red eyes. A dozen riders on black horses drew up before him. The leader chilled my sap. A massive figure with a dark face and antlers sharp as knives.

"Bréanainn, knight of the Bright Court," said the Horned One. "We seek a mortal who has dared to enter our realm."

Brendan stood and inclined his head. "Lord of the Wild Hunt, good fortune to you."

"Do you know aught of whom we seek?"

"I saw a mortal maiden at the faerie ring this morning," Brendan said, perfectly truthfully, "but she disappeared before I could detain her and drag her to my liege."

The Horned One's steed pawed the earth just beyond the reach of my roots.

"She is not here," he stated.

Brendan gazed around the meadow. "I see no mortal maid."

"Indeed." The Horned One studied Brendan for a moment. "Ride on," he commanded his huntsmen. "We'll seek elsewhere for the human." And with that both pack and riders surged away, riding not across the meadow, but into the sky where they disappeared among the clouds.

Brendan waited for a long moment before turning to my tree. "Return to your natural form, Emma. You are safe now."

I released the oak spell and transformed into my Feyland self.

Brendan caught me when I stumbled and would have fallen. He hugged me tight, then held me at arms length. "Your spell should work now, little one. It would be best for you to return to the mortal realm."

I nodded my agreement, still a bit sluggish from my stint as a tree.

"Dare I hope that you will come again?" he asked.

"Oh, yes," I answered with a smile. "I'll definitely be back." My smile faded. "But how will you know when I come? How will we find each other?"

He pulled a golden chain from beneath his shirt and unclasped it. "Please," he said. "Accept my token. As long as you wear this talisman, I shall find you. Anywhere. Even in the mortal realm, though I have never sought to enter that fell land."

He placed the chain around my neck and I touched the fili-greed pendant that dangled from it before tucking it inside my tunic.

"I'll wear it always."

"Lest you be alarmed," he said with a smile, and again it seemed like the day brightened, "be aware that this talisman will manifest only in the Realm of Faerie. You will not see it in the human world, or even in the game you think you play, but unless you remove it here, it will remain with you and will mark you so that I may find you."

I nodded. "I understand." I didn't, not really, but I could see that Brendan believed his words, so I accepted his belief.

He raised my hand to his lips and kissed my knuckle. "Safe travels, Lady Emma."

I smiled, embarrassed, but incredibly happy. "And to you, Sir Brendan." Withdrawing my hand from his, I murmured, "Deac-tivate Feyland."

4

---

*D*ad and Uncle Jim and Jennet and I sat in the conservatory where I could use Uncle Jim's special grav chair and interface which allowed me to speak. We'd finished dinner —a rather tedious affair for me since I couldn't communicate and my nurse had to feed me — and were discussing Feyland. I raved about the game, praising the interface and Uncle Jim's amazing work. Jennet looked at me a little strangely from time to time, but it was so nice to be able to talk to her at long last that I didn't worry about it.

Finally, Dad and Uncle Jim went to the library so Uncle Jim could use Dad's computer to show him the screenie version of Feyland. Dad was so excited about me being able to use the game that he was thinking about buying a Full-D gaming system for himself so we could play together.

That sounded great to me. I wanted Dad to see me as my Feyland self, and I wanted to introduce him to Brendan. Dad wouldn't have to know that Brendan wasn't just another teenager playing a game. Some things were better left unsaid, and I knew Brendan would understand. Faeries are masters of illusion.

Jennet scooted her chair closer to me and said, "Did, uhm, anything unusual happen to you while you were in-game?"

"Unusual?" I asked, hoping my computer voice sounded innocent. "Like what?"

"Well," she said, glancing around to make sure we were still alone. "I couldn't help but notice a certain, well, *glow* about you. I mean, I know you're excited by how realistic the game is, and how it allows you to walk and talk and everything, but still..." She paused, licked her lips, and then blurted, "You just seem, I don't know, different."

I blinked. First she asked if anything unusual had happened in the game, and then she noticed a difference about me, a *glow*? Could it have anything to do with Brendan's talisman?

"Well," I said. "I made a friend. A boy." If I'd been capable of blushing, I'm sure I would've turned bright red.

"A boy, huh?" She smiled, relief evident in her expression. How odd. "What character class was he playing?"

"That was kind of strange," I said, watching my cousin for a reaction. Jennet was an expert on Feyland. If there was such a thing as the Realm of Faerie, I was willing to bet she knew about it. "He said he was a faerie knight, but I didn't see that classification when I chose to be a dryad. Do more choices open up when you get to the higher levels?"

Jennet's face paled, and even though she quickly clasped her hands, I noticed a slight trembling.

"No," she said quietly. "The character classes don't change." She licked her lips again and then asked, "What else did he say?"

"Well, he told me he wasn't human and that he was part of some court, and was supposed to take stray humans to see the king." Jennet's face went paler still, but I kept going. "Honestly, I didn't know what to think, except that he seemed to believe what he was saying. Was it all just part of the game, Jennet?"

My cousin shook her head, took a deep breath and exhaled slowly, her eyes closed. When she opened them, her color looked better. "No, it's not part of the game. Not at all. The Realm of Faerie is very real, Emma, and it can be dangerous. If your new friend told you he's a faerie knight, he probably is."

I blinked, gathering my thoughts before willing my mechanical voice to speak. "I guess I should tell you about the talisman, then."

Jennet narrowed her eyes. "What talisman?"

"The necklace. He gave me a necklace and said it would mark me ... that as long as I wore it, he'd be able to find me. Anywhere. Even here."

"Oh, Emma." Jennet closed her eyes and almost moaned. "Tell me you didn't accept it."

For the millionth time, I wished I could move my head, wished I could nod my agreement. But of course, even if I could move, I wouldn't have been able to do that. I *had* accepted the necklace.

"No," I said, my new voice firmer and more confident than I felt. "I accepted it. I'd show it to you, but he said I wouldn't be able to see it in this world ... or even in the game."

She reached forward and touched my cheek, staring straight into my eyes. "Promise me you won't go back into the game without me. You can't risk finding yourself back in Faerie without backup."

I hesitated. I wanted to visit Feyland again as soon as possible, even with everything Jennet had said. I'd been frightened when the Wild Hunt appeared, but I'd never felt threatened by Brendan. I really wanted to see him again. But Jennet definitely seemed to understand things I didn't and much as I wanted to experience a fully functional body again, I wasn't interested in endangering myself.

Unfortunately, Jennet and her dad were just visiting. Her

Full-D system was at her home in Crestview. I had no idea how long they intended to stay. How long was she asking me to wait?

My cousin seemed to read my mind.

"I know I'm asking a lot," Jennet said, gazing so intently into my eyes that I wondered if she really could read my mind. "I can't imagine what it must be like to finally be free of that chair, to be able to move on your own and talk without assistance. I'm sure you want to go back into the game as soon as possible."

She laid her hand, her strong capable hand, over my withered one and stroked my fingers. I couldn't feel her touch, but I saw the movement and read the compassion in her eyes.

"We don't know each other as well as we should, Emma," she said quietly. "Stuff has always come between us." Her eyes flicked from the bands holding my upper body in place to the grav chair and back to my face. "But I need you to trust me in this. Faerie is a dangerous place. There are things I need to tell you, stuff I need to explain, and it'll be easier if we're in-game when I do it. Will you wait for me, Emma?"

I blinked twice, then remembered I could speak. "I do trust you, Jennet. Your dad has given me a miracle. I can wait a few days to experience more."

She nodded. "Thank you, Emma. I'll call as soon as we're home and we can meet in Feyland." She grinned and her eyes sparkled with excitement. "I can't wait to see your dryad character and to have some real girl time, just the two of us. It's going to be mag, playing the game together!"

5

*T*he next few days were the longest of my life.

Okay. That's not true. I'd endured much longer hospital stays, including ones that had centered on horrifically painful testing. I was no stranger to discomfort. But this wasn't about pain. This was about excitement and anticipation. I longed to return to Feyland, to the freedom I enjoyed there. But I'd promised Jennet I'd wait, so wait I did.

I had long conversations with Dad, my nurse, my physical therapist, anyone who would stand still long enough to hear about the wonders of Feyland and how awesome my uncle was to have made it possible for me to play and, no less importantly, to talk! But I resisted the urge to enter the game alone.

Finally. FINALLY, Jennet called and Dad gave me the time she'd arranged for us to meet in-game. I stared at the clock across the conservatory, and the instant the second hand hit the appointed time, I thought, *Enter Feyland!*

When the opening screens cleared, I stood inside the ring of mushrooms in a familiar clearing surrounded by white-barked trees with silver leaves, and Jennet stood just outside the circle. At least I thought it was Jennet. She looked a little imposing in her long, blue Spellweaver robes, her blonde hair covered by the hood, and leaning on a mage staff.

We stared at each other for a moment, each coming to terms with the changes in the other's appearance. Jennet broke our self-imposed silence.

"Oh my god, Emma! Is that really you?"

I grinned and twirled around inside the circle of mushrooms. "It's me," I cried, "and I can stand and walk and run and dance ... and talk with my own mouth and vocal chords! Isn't this the best?"

Her eyes brimmed with tears. "You're beautiful," she whispered. "I mean, you are in the real world too," she wiped her cheeks as a few tears escaped, "but ...."

"Yeah, I know," my own voice sounded a bit husky, "it's hard to see past the facial tics and grimaces that I can't control and all the straps and stuff holding me in place."

"Oh, Emma!" She stepped across the mushrooms and pulled me into a tight hug. "Your dad is going to flip when he sees you here. You're absolutely glowing with joy."

We parted and both of us wiped our eyes. I sniffled a bit, then sucked in a breath, and marshaling my emotions, asked, "So what was so important that we had to talk in Feyland?"

Jennet dabbed her eyes one last time with the sleeve of her robe, straightened and said, "Right. Warnings first, then we can play. First up, take a good look around. Do you see anything different this time? Anything that doesn't look the same as the times you entered the game alone?"

"Besides you being here?"

She cocked an eyebrow at me with a *Well, duh* expression on her face.

I grinned, ducked my head and immediately noticed a difference. "The mushrooms," I cried. "They're brown!"

"They haven't been before?"

"No. Both the other times I landed in a circle of red mushrooms with little white spots."

She nodded and released the breath she'd been holding. "Okay. That's your trigger. When you play the game on your own, if the mushrooms are red and white, leave immediately and try again later. If they're brown, like these, it's safe to play."

"Seriously?"

"Seriously. The circle of red caps indicates that you've landed in Faerie instead of Feyland."

Jennet stepped out of the circle of innocent brown mushrooms and I followed. "That's a relief," she said.

"What is?"

"That the mushroom circle holds true. When you went straight to Faerie on both your first two attempts at the game, I was afraid you'd stumbled across a thin spot we weren't aware of."

"Who's 'we' and what's a thin spot?"

"We're the Feyguard. We've been appointed by the Old Ones to guard the borders between our world and the Realm of Faerie and rescue humans who stumble across unaware."

"Like me."

"Exactly like you," Jennet said with a nod. "But no one else has ever been marked so that they could be traced into our world. That talisman you accepted really worries me."

I touched the place Brendan's talisman rested. Even though I couldn't see it, I knew it was there. "He said I was special," I said, half to myself. I looked up at Jennet. "Do you think he meant it?"

"You are special, Emma," she said, her voice full of ... I wasn't sure what, but I thought it might be respect. Not something I'd had much experience with. "In so many ways." She gave me a one-armed hug, and said, "What can you tell me about your friend?"

"Well, he told me his name..."

"He *WHAT*?" Jennet yelped.

"Yeah," I said with a smile. "I've read enough fairy tales to know that's significant too."

While we talked, we strolled along a path strewn with tiny white flowers, beneath the arching branches of those lovely white-barked trees. Their silver leaves rustled in the breeze, reminding me of the bamboo wind chimes that hung in our garden at home. I told Jennet everything that had happened in my first two visits to Feyland, or rather, as I now knew, to the Realm of Faerie. The only thing I left out was Brendan's name. He'd given that to *me*. If he wanted Jennet to know it, he'd have to tell her himself. She seemed to understand. At least, she didn't press me on that point.

"And he pledged to protect you?" she asked, a puzzled frown on her pretty face.

I nodded. "I trust him, Jennet," I said quietly as we stepped into a clearing that led down to a little stream. Very little. Barely more than a trickle of water.

My eyes widened in surprise and I grabbed Jennet's arm. "There he is!"

Her head whipped up and she gazed at the trees behind us. "He can't be. We're not in Faerie. We're in the game. I was very careful!"

I pointed, and she turned to look toward the rivulet.

Brendan stood just beyond the trickle of water that barely qualified as a stream. A soft heat-haze shimmered around him as he raised a hand, palm out, in greeting.

"Oh!" Jennet exclaimed, as I practically ran to meet him. "Emma! Stop!" she cried. "Don't cross the running water."

I stopped just short of the stream. It was so narrow and shallow that it wasn't much of a barrier, but if Jennet didn't want me to cross, I wouldn't.

"I'm so glad to see you," I said to Brendan. "I wondered if you'd come."

"It is hard for me to enter your game," he said. "It is part of the mortal realm and therefore foreign to me. I cannot stay but a moment. I haven't the strength."

Jennet approached cautiously.

I nodded toward her. "This is my cousin," I told him. "I've been telling her about our adventures, but I haven't mentioned names." I laughed, a bit nervously. "It makes introductions a little awkward."

He smiled and bowed to Jennet. "I recognize you, Guardian," he said. "You need have no fear. I mean your cousin no harm. She has become dear to me."

Jennet returned his bow. "Thank you, sir knight, that relieves my mind." A small frown creased her brow. "How have you come here?"

Brendan glanced at me. "She carries my talisman. It calls me. But I haven't the strength to remain. Farewell, my friend," he said with a smile. "I look forward to our next meeting."

He vanished, and so did the measly little stream.

Jennet collapsed on the flower strewn grass. "Okay. That was weird."

"Was it?" I settled beside her. "I'm so glad he came. Now you've seen for yourself that he's not a bad guy."

"No," she said, "he's not a bad guy and he genuinely seems to like you, maybe even care about you." She shivered, sat a little straighter, and looked me square in the eye. "But you still have to be careful, Emma. Promise me you won't stray beyond Feyland. Not even to see him. Promise me you'll leave immediately if the mushrooms are red."

Her expression was so fierce that I licked my lips. I didn't want to lie to my cousin, and I didn't want to endanger myself or any of her Feyguard friends, but I didn't want to lose Brendan's friendship either. He was, after all, the first friend I'd ever had.

"Emma…"

I buried my hand in my tunic, crossed my fingers, and said, "Fine. Okay. I promise."

And I meant it. Sort of. At least for now. But I had an out if circumstances should ever require me to break that promise.

For now, I'd be content to play the game. To use Feyland to get to know Jennet better — and possibly my own father! — and I'd be happy with brief glimpses of Brendan. After all, it was more, so much more, than I'd ever had before.

But if a time ever came when Brendan needed my help, I'd act without a second thought. No one had ever needed anything from me before, and I'd never had anything to give, so if the opportunity arose, I promised myself I'd grab it and not let go.

"So," Jennet's voice broke into my slightly rebellious thoughts — something else I'd never had the capacity for, rebellion! — and I turned my attention to the here and now. "Do you want to, you know, actually play the game?"

I grinned and grabbed her hand. "You bet! Lead on, cousin. I want to learn everything there is to know about Feyland." *And maybe Faerie as well*, I added to myself. No need to let Jennet know just how rebellious I was prepared to become…

COPYRIGHT

AWAKENING THE WARRIOR

PROLOGUE

arbird Pilot Caleb Leaping Trout stood at attention in the corridor of Absaroka's flagship. He fixed his gaze on the blank wall opposite him, trying not to see the death of his career in its smooth white surface. The Bug-Eye crisis had passed, no thanks to him, and the time had come for him to answer for his foolishness.

He longed to loosen the stranglehold of his dress uniform's collar, but knew better than to relax his formal stance. He was in enough trouble without giving his superior officers additional evidence of his unsuitability to remain a pilot in Absaroka's defense fleet.

Warchief Brenna Standing Bear was dead because of him, and her people, *his* people, mourned her loss, while thanking the Great Spirit for her courage.

He swallowed, tasting bile. He knew he wasn't actually responsible for the warchief's death, but he also knew that if he'd been at the controls of his warbird ... if he'd been sober and flying the *Falcon* in battle as he should have been, she wouldn't have been able to commandeer his ship and sacrifice herself for the defense of Absaroka.

It should have been him.

Warchief Standing Bear should have ordered him to test her theory. She should never have been in the *Falcon*. Caleb Leaping Trout should have died, not his warchief.

1

―――――

"Come on, Caleb," wheedled Jeremy Wolfclaw. "You know you could fly those stupid readiness exercises with one hand tied behind your back."

"Sorry, Jer. My duty..."

"Your *duty* is to your best friend! Bro, I'm getting *married* tomorrow. I need you at my side tonight. You're my, what do you call it? Oh, yeah. You're my *wingman*! You gotta come, Caleb. Tomorrow's too late. Tomorrow night I'll be busy making little Wolfclaws with Simone." Jeremy wiggled his eyebrows suggestively and clapped Caleb on the back. "Come on, man. You can't let a brother down in his hour of need."

Caleb shook his head, then grinned at his best friend. "I don't know how you managed to get a beauty like Simone to agree to marry you, but yeah, I'll celebrate with you tonight." He paused for a moment, studying his friend's honest, but somewhat homely face. Jeremy was a good man, but he didn't understand Caleb's responsibility to the fleet, or the command structure he answered to. Jeremy was a code-cruncher. He sat in a cubicle all day. The worst thing he ever wrestled with was a snarly tangle of bits and bytes.

The two guys might have grown up together, but their adult lives were worlds apart.

But Jeremy was right about one thing: Caleb could fly readiness exercises blindfolded. He could afford to go out drinking with his best friend tonight. After all, the exercises would force him to miss Jeremy's wedding, so this was his only chance to toast his friend's happiness.

Besides, the Bug-Eyes had turned tail and run before either of them had been born. The readiness exercises, hell, the whole planetary defense fleet, was a product of Warchief Standing Bear's family paranoia. Not that he minded. If there wasn't a defense fleet, he wouldn't be a pilot, and the one thing Caleb Leaping Trout knew for sure was that he'd been born to fly a warbird.

2

———

*C*aleb woke to a shrill sound drilling a hole in his head. He yanked a pillow over his ears and applied pressure, trying to make sure his skull didn't explode.

"Alarm off!" he yelled into his bedroom's dim light. The noise ceased and he released the pillow and flopped onto his back. Great Spirit! His head throbbed, his eyes were gritty, and his stomach churned. What had happened to him last night?

He lay still, hoping his body would settle, and his bedroom would stop shimmying and shaking. Closing his eyes, he tried to think. Tried to remember what he'd done last night. Flying lug nuts, dredging up memories hurt! He pressed his hands to his eyes to hold his brain in place while he searched for answers.

Jeremy. Drinking. Celebrating. More drinking.

Right. He'd gone out with Jeremy and the two of them had experimented with every intoxicant they could find in Tahlequah's club district. And Absaroka's capital city had a lot of clubs and a galaxy's worth of liquor.

Caleb smiled ruefully. He hoped Jeremy was in better shape than he was. After all, Jer was getting married this morning, and

Simone wouldn't be impressed if her groom couldn't stand up for the ceremony.

Awareness came flooding back, and Caleb jerked to sitting. His head swam and his stomach lurched, but he didn't have time to acknowledge the pain. He had readiness exercises this morning. He had to get dressed and get to his warbird. If he failed to show, he'd be in the brig before Jeremy managed to mutter "I do."

Two hours later, Caleb sat strapped into the pilot's seat in the *Falcon*. He'd launched from the *Thunderbird's* flight deck in formation with the rest of his shroud of five warbirds, and now struggled to maintain his position in the intricate drills his shroud leader commanded.

Sweat dripped from the end of his nose, fogging the faceplate of his helmet. This should've been easy. His shroud had practiced these maneuvers until he could manipulate the controls in his sleep. But today his head throbbed, his muscles ached, and he knew his responses were sluggish. He gritted his teeth and wished he could yank off his helmet and wipe the damn faceplate. He had enough trouble focusing his bloodshot eyes without trying to peer through the condensation of his own sweat.

Static crackled over his communication array. "Pilot Leaping Trout," the voice said. Caleb frowned. A man's voice. Not his shroud leader Jenny Lightfoot's clear tones. "This is Chief of the Deck Black Bear. Return to the *Thunderbird*. Now."

"Aye, shir," Caleb said, his words slurring as his stomach gave a queasy roll. "Jush le' me inform..."

"Now, Pilot Leaping Trout," the COD said sharply. "Your shroud leader has already been informed."

"Aye, shir. Returnin' now."

One less than perfect landing later, Caleb climbed

unsteadily from the *Falcon* and swayed to attention on the flight deck as the COD approached.

"Just what do you think you were doing out there, Pilot Leaping Trout?" the COD growled.

"Followin' orders, shir," Caleb answered, his words slurring even more now that he was face to face with his superior officer.

"I don't think so, mister," barked the COD. "You've been sluggish answering your hails and sloppy with the formations." He stopped, leaned toward the young pilot and then backed away quickly. "And you stink of whiskey. That's it. You're grounded, and confined to quarters until Chief Whitehorse has time to deal with you. Dismissed."

"Bu...but..." Caleb sputtered.

"I said, 'Dismissed,' Pilot Leaping Trout. Do you need me to draw you a picture?" The COD leaned close and glared at the younger man.

"No shir ... I mean, yesh shir," he said, confused. Not sure what response was required, Caleb saluted, or tried to, and stumbled away from the COD and back to his shipboard quarters.

Great Spirit! What had he done? Why had he allowed himself to drink so much last night? Why hadn't he accompanied Jeremy on his night out, but limited himself to a single toast? Why in the name of all his revered ancestors had he matched Jeremy drink for drink?

If he lost the *Falcon* ... if he was dishonorably discharged .... It didn't bear thinking about.

He reached his quarters and shut himself in, only vaguely aware of the airmen who'd followed him and now stood guard at his door. He was in deep shit. But his head throbbed and every muscle in his body ached. Chief Whitehorse wouldn't have time to discipline him until after the exercises, so he might as well try to sleep it off.

He shrugged out of his boots and flight suit and collapsed on his bunk. Maybe when he woke up he'd discover this was all a bad dream.

3

—————

*B*ut it wasn't a dream. It was a nightmare.

Caleb woke to a clear head, calm stomach, and muscle aches that he knew would succumb to a couple of pain tablets, but his world was in turmoil. Code Red lights flashed and shrill sirens drilled into his ears. He raced barefoot to the door, yanked it open and met an armed guard.

"Remain in your quarters, Pilot Leaping Trout," the man said, eyeing him with disgust.

Caleb raised his hands and took a step away from the door. "What's happening? Is this a drill?"

"It is not. We're under attack," the man growled. "Bug-Eyes." His eyes flicked over Caleb. "And I'm stuck guarding a pilot who's too drunk to be of use."

"Bug-Eyes?" Caleb asked in disbelief. "But that can't be right. They disappeared decades ago!"

"They're back," the guard said, and closed the door in Caleb's face.

Stunned, Caleb stood rooted to the deck of *Thunderbird*, marooned in his quarters. Barefoot, wearing only a tee-shirt and shorts. The siren and flashing lights faded from his awareness, his thoughts spiraling. He should be out there. He should be in the cockpit of the *Falcon*, fighting Bug-Eyes with his shroud.

Great Spirit! His shroud! Jenny and John and Anna and David were out there deploying the maneuvers they'd practiced, but they were a man short ... a warbird short. He'd left a hole in their formations. He'd left his shroud at a disadvantage, weakened. He'd failed his people in their hour of need.

And for what? To celebrate with Jeremy?

Jeremy and Simone might not even survive if the Bug-Eyes broke through the fleet's defenses ... and Caleb had weakened those defenses.

He'd failed. He wasn't a warrior. He was a spoiled child who put his own wants above his responsibilities to his shroud ... to his fleet ... to his people.

Caleb Leaping Trout sank onto his bunk, his head in his hands.

If he made it off the *Thunderbird*, if the *Thunderbird* survived the battle, his military career was over, and he'd richly deserve whatever punishment Chief Whitehorse and Warchief Standing Bear doled out.

4

The crisis passed. The *Thunderbird*, the fleet's flagship, survived. Two of the fleet's five destroyers, the *Choctaw* and the *Seminole*, did not. The fleet also lost three cruisers, the *Kiowa*, the *Lakota*, and the *Ute*. But most devastating to Caleb was the loss his warbird, the *Falcon*.

His shroud leader, Jenny Lightfoot, took pity on him and visited him in his quarters to bring him up to speed. Jenny and Caleb were the only remaining members of their shroud of five warbirds, and his fighter craft was destroyed as well.

"From what I understand," Jenny said, sitting crossed legged on the floor beside him, "Warchief Standing Bear commandeered the *Falcon* to test a theory. Whatever that weapon was that they were using against us, it simply disintegrated our ships. The *Choctaw* and the *Seminole* didn't stand a chance against it. The beam touched them, and they imploded."

She shook her head. "It was horrible. The Bug-Eye fighters were bad enough, but that weapon ... it was unbeatable."

"But what happened to the warchief," Caleb asked, when what he really meant was, what happened to the *Falcon*?

"Right. Well, the story that's making the rounds is that she noticed that the ship seemed vulnerable while it was recharging, and rather than ordering one of us, one of the remaining warbirds, to ram the ship, she commandeered the *Falcon* and did it herself."

Jenny shook her head. "She timed it perfectly. No pilot could've done better. She waited until the ship was just about to deploy that terrifying energy and then rammed the *Falcon* right down the maw of that weapon. The thing backfired and the Bug-Eye ship and the *Falcon* imploded together."

The two pilots sat in silence, pondering the courage and quick thinking of their warchief. After a moment, Jenny shook herself and continued. "Once the big ship was gone, the rest was just a mop-up exercise. The Bug-Eye fighters had nowhere to go. Our remaining warbirds and cruisers picked them off easily."

She sighed. "We won. Absaroka is safe and the USL has been warned, but..."

"But the cost was high," Caleb said, finishing her thought. "I'm sorry, Jenny. I know that's not enough. Nothing I do will be enough. But I am sorry. I let you and the others down." He drew a shuddering breath. "And John and Anna and David paid with their lives."

Jenny touched his knee. "I'm not condoning what you did," she said quietly, "but don't beat yourself up. Yes, you were wrong and you'll deserve whatever punishment the chief decides is warranted, but you couldn't have known ... none of us could ... it was just supposed to be an exercise. No one was supposed to die."

Caleb swallowed past the lump in this throat and averted his eyes. She was right. He knew she was right. But how was he supposed to live with the guilt?

EPILOGUE

*W*arbird Pilot Caleb Leaping Trout stood at attention in the corridor outside Warchief Whitehorse's private office. The moment of truth had arrived. He raised his chin, ignoring the itch of the rarely worn dress uniform, the stiffness of the collar that tried to choke him. Whatever came, he deserved. His failure was unforgivable.

The office door opened with a soft "whoosh" and the Warchief's first officer stepped out. His gaze raked Caleb from head to toe before he spoke. "Warchief Whitehorse will see you now."

Caleb saluted crisply. "Aye, sir." He strode into the office to meet his fate, back straight, shoulders square. The door whooshed closed behind him as he saluted his newly appointed warchief.

Alex Whitehorse looked up from the tactical display covering the surface of his desk and said, "At ease, Pilot Leaping Trout."

Caleb released his salute and assumed a parade rest stance, gaze fastened on the wall behind the warchief's head. Though he maintained a stoic facial expression, Caleb was shocked by

Whitehorse's appearance. The man looked like he had aged decades in the week since Caleb had last seen him.

"Caleb Leaping Trout, you have been charged with incapacitation of duty due to indulgence. What do you have to say for yourself?"

"Sir. I have no defense. I overindulged the night before our readiness exercises, being fully aware of the importance of the next day's events. Despite a severe hangover, I reported for duty and took my warbird out. The COD was forced to call me in due to my poor performance, leaving my shroud at a disadvantage."

Caleb paused. He closed his eyes and his shoulders slumped. After a moment, he opened his eyes again and met his warchief's gaze. "When I came to in my quarters and realized we were under attack...." He licked his lips. "Sir, I'm deeply ashamed. I don't deserve to be called a warrior. I left my shroud in a weakened state and contributed to the deaths of my fellow pilots. I acknowledge my guilt and accept any consequences you see fit to impose, though nothing will erase my culpability."

Warchief Whitehorse studied Caleb, his gaze seeming to penetrate to the pilot's soul. After a long moment, he spoke.

"I believe you speak honestly, Pilot Leaping Trout. You had no way of knowing that a scheduled exercise would turn into a full-scale battle, though that is exactly what readiness exercises are designed to do: prepare us for battle. Ensure that we're ready for the real thing."

Whitehorse sighed and scrubbed a hand over his face. "We lost a lot of good men and women in that battle," he said wearily. "And frankly, I can't afford to lose an able pilot over what should have been a simple case of drunkenness."

He stood, leaned across his desk, hands splayed on the tactical display. "I want to believe that this experience has awakened you to the importance of your duty, son. Has it?"

Caleb nodded, his jaw tight. With a conscious effort he

relaxed enough to answer. "It has, sir. I am awake and aware of my duty to my people. My warbird carried Brenna Standing Bear to her death ... and to the salvation of Absaroka. I will do everything in my power to be worthy of her sacrifice."

Whitehorse nodded. "Very well. You are grounded until the COD releases you for flight. Until that time you will work with the ground crew assuring that all warbirds are fully functional and ready for battle. Are your orders clear?"

Caleb snapped to attention and saluted. "Aye, sir. Thank you, sir."

"You are dismissed, pilot."

Caleb executed a precise military turn and exited the warchief's office. Once he rounded a corner and was out of sight of the door, he slumped against the wall. Closing his eyes, he pictured his fallen friends, and apologizing inwardly, bade each farewell. When he opened his eyes, he shook himself, straightened his shoulders, and went to find the COD and report for ground duty, determined to be the best warrior in the fleet. To be worthy of his warchief's leniency ... and Brenna Standing Bear's sacrifice.

INCIDENT ON THE ODYSSEY

1

Captain Caren Fielding stood on the bridge of *USL Odyssey*, a Universal Star League deep space exploratory vessel.

Her ship. Her bridge. Her responsibility.

She presented herself to her crew as an exemplary USL officer should: spotless blue and silver uniform, dark hair pulled into a tight knot at the base of her neck, face calm, controlled.

Everything regulation. Everything by the book.

Everything except the phantom stink of blood and human waste.

She controlled a grimace, refused to acknowledge the bile rising in her throat. The odor was a delusion. She knew it. The cleaning bots had worked through the night, removing all trace of the bodies that had exploded on her watch yesterday.

Blake's body.

Momentarily closing her eyes, she drew a deep breath, forcing herself to catalog the room's actual scents. Harsh chemical cleaning compounds stung her nostrils, overlaid with a clean, salty tang someone had named *ocean breeze*. Caren had never been near an ocean — neither had anyone else on this vessel—so she had no idea if the scent was accurate, but at least it wasn't the sweetly rotten melding of burned flesh, blood and feces.

She opened her eyes, observed the immaculately clean surfaces surrounding her people. Spotless white plasteel walls, gleaming chrome work surfaces, structural seating in a deep USL blue. Her crew's uniforms were equally squared away, their blues crisply pressed with polished silver rank insignia.

Clasping her hands behind her back, Caren listened to the familiar sounds of her bridge. The soft murmur of voices, both human and computer sim, set against the deep hum of engines — felt as much as heard — and the nearly inaudible *whoosh* of air cycling through the ventilation system.

Satisfied, she moved from station to station, monitoring her crew's work. Prowling as silently as a cat, nodding to those who made eye contact, murmuring encouragement to those who did not. Quietly evaluating the state of her bridge, the level of distress among her people.

They were a good crew, these eleven officers. Nine of them had been on the bridge with her last night. Only Perkins and Tse had escaped the horror. The night shift — those officers who had relieved her crew after the *incident* — had taken their watch on the auxiliary bridge. Cleaning bots had maintained sole possession of this space over what passed for night on the deep-space ship.

Caren returned to the command position and lowered herself into the captain's chair. Normally the chair molded to her form, suspending her body and enfolding her arms and hands so that her slightest movement registered against the ship's controls. Today she didn't allow it. She sat stiffly, rigidly erect. On guard. She would brook no comfort, no relaxation. Perhaps if she'd been more vigilant, less at ease, Blake would still be beside her, still be her steady right hand. An excellent first officer ... and her perfect mate.

She pushed the thought away. Blake was dead. She should know; she'd been covered in his remains, bathed in his blood.

He hadn't died alone. Ensign Jordan Whittaker had gone down as well. Now Lieutenant Perkins stood at Blake's station and Ensign Tse monitored Whittaker's controls. Life went on. The ship went on. And it was Caren's duty to move on as well.

Blake would expect that of her.

But Blake would never know the courage that seemingly simple task required.

Moving on. It sounded so easy, but it took every atom of her self-discipline not to run screaming from this place. Her bridge, the place she'd felt most competent, most in control, now felt like a tomb; a monument to Blake and Whittaker. No longer an efficient place where life went on and duty was fulfilled.

She stood again and, using her most controlled command voice, addressed the bridge crew. "If I could have your attention." She paused while every officer in the room turned to face her. She made brief eye contact with each one before continuing. "I know you're all distressed by what happened yesterday. I certainly am, but we need to continue to function in an efficient and capable manner. Our engineering crew and our technical programmers assure me that yesterday's *incident*, while regrettable, was a fluke, that we are in no more danger on this bridge than anywhere else on the ship. While we don't yet know what caused the deaths of Commander Larsen and Ensign Whittaker, we do know that we were not attacked — there are no other ships in our vicinity. We also know that none of our own systems malfunctioned."

Caren scanned her crew again, looking for signs of overt fear or distress. She found none. Deep sadness, yes; concern and confusion, yes; but not fear.

"We will continue to study the ... *incident*. We will discover the cause of the deaths. But we can only accomplish this task if everyone is alert and on guard.

"If any of you feel incapable of working in this environment, report to Lieutenant Perkins. He will relieve you, make arrangements for counseling, and arrange for another officer to assume your duties." She glanced at Perkins, who nodded his understanding.

"No one will think less of you for admitting to being traumatized," she said, her voice quieter, a bit less stern. "However, if you choose to remain at your station, you will be expected to function competently and without hesitation. Are there any questions?"

Her question was met with a low chorus of "No, sir."

She nodded. "Very well. You may resume your duties."

As her officers returned to their screens and controls, Caren moved to stand behind her captain's chair, hands resting lightly on its headrest. Catching Perkins' eye, she motioned for him to join her.

When he stood before her, one eyebrow slightly raised in query, she said, "You have the conn. I'll be in my ready room, if you need me. I want to review the techs' findings. Keep me apprised of the crew's state of readiness."

Perkins nodded. "Of course, Captain Fielding."

2

---

*C*aren's ready room had always been a refuge. A place where she could relax, away from the assessing eyes of the crew and the expectations of command. Unlike the cold white and chrome of the bridge, her ready room boasted walls of a soft blue, its plasteel furnishings hidden beneath a veneer that mimicked Old Earth oak. Sinking into the padded desk chair, she relaxed, appreciating the way its perfectly proportioned contours cupped her body, enjoying the comforting familiarity of its tawny faux leather.

She closed her eyes and sighed deeply, allowing herself a moment to feel the fear and trauma of the unexplained deaths. Danger was inherent in space travel, especially aboard an exploratory vessel. She and her crew lived with the unknown. They plumbed its depths on a daily basis.

But an unexplained death ... something that snuffed out life in such a random manner ... without raising an alarm ... something that attacked life in the most secure environment on the ship ... this was intolerable. The *incident* had to be explained! The danger had to be identified, the threat categorized.

Exploring the unknown was acceptable simply because

everyone knew that once it was encountered, it would become known.

She opened her eyes and straightened in her chair.

Trauma and grief would have to wait. There was work to be done.

Blake and Whittaker had died. That was unassailable fact. The manner of their death was part of the ship's record. It was up to her to determine the cause. The unknown must become known for the safety and sanity of her crew ... and every other crew that ventured into this region of space.

She activated her work station, and got on with it.

Caren was studying the various reports from the time of the incident when the door to the bridge *whooshed* open and Lieutenant Perkins stepped through.

"Excuse me, Captain, but there have been several more deaths."

Caren froze, then fisted her hands on the simulated oak desk and snapped, "Report!"

Perkins straightened, clasped his hands behind his back, and stared at a spot just beyond Caren's left shoulder.

"The deaths were all identical to Larsen and Whittaker. One in engineering, one in hydroponics, and one in the medical bay."

Caren stood and paced from one end of the room to the other.

"And there are no signs of a ship? Could it be cloaked? Using technology we don't understand?"

"Nothing has been detected, sir." Perkins paused a moment before continuing. "However, Dr. Okeke from research reported an anomaly."

Caren rounded on him. "What anomaly?"

"She's a physicist, sir. Her verbal report ... well, much of it went over my head." He scrunched his shoulders as though trying to protect the deficient part of his anatomy. Evidently admitting his lack of understanding embarrassed the young officer.

Caren skewered him with her best commanding officer gaze, and he straightened and continued.

"My take was that she saw something in the data that supported an Old Earth theory that has never been proved. Something about emissions from a neutron star. I caught a phrase or two, but you're going to need to hear her findings for yourself."

"Very well," Caren said. "Return to the bridge and do what you can to keep the crew calm and functioning. I'll speak to Dr. Okeke."

Lieutenant Perkins executed a precise military turn, strode to the door, which *whooshed* open at his approach, and disappeared onto the bridge.

The instant the door closed, Caren turned to the viewscreen opposite her desk and contacted the research division. A very young, very pallid man wearing a white lab coat appeared on screen.

"This is Captain Fielding," Caren said before the young man could speak. "Get me Dr. Okeke immediately."

The young researcher's jaw dropped open, his eyes widened. He looked in danger of fainting.

"Now!" Caren snapped.

"Sir ... yes, sir," he squeaked.

Caren drummed her fingers on her desk as she watched the young man dodge and weave out of camera range. A few moments (that felt like hours!) later, a very dark skinned woman with high cheekbones and a cap of sleek black hair appeared on the viewscreen.

"Captain Fielding," she said, her voice calm and melodic. "I am Dr. Chi Okeke. I presume this is in regard to the report I gave to your first officer."

"It is. Thank you for speaking to me, Doctor. Lt. Perkins' summary was rather bare bones. What can you tell me?"

Dr. Okeke nodded, her expression serious, but excitement gleamed in her eyes. "I ... we ... noted some anomalous readings in the data from yesterday evening and again this morning. Readings we've never encountered before, but that correspond to theories raised on Earth in the late twentieth century."

She paused, closed her eyes, took a deep breath, and continued. "We believe we've encountered *exotic hadrons*, *hexaquarks* to be exact." Her eyes flew open, shining with elation. "They seem to be emanating from the neutron star we detected two days ago."

Caren nodded. "I can see that you're excited, Dr. Okeke, but does this have anything to do with the unexplained deaths we're experiencing?"

Dr. Okeke frowned. "Our findings are too preliminary to make such an assumption, Captain. We were only asked to report any unusual readings."

Caren sighed and rubbed her temple. "I sympathize with your need for empirical evidence, doctor. But our people are dying and I don't know what's killing them or how to protect them. These *hexaquarks* of yours are the only anomaly we've discovered. Is there any way for you to determine if they are the cause? And if they are, can you find a way to prevent further casualties?"

"We'll do our best, Captain. I'll keep you informed of our progress. Dr. Okeke out."

Caren's viewscreen went blank.

3

The next few hours wreaked havoc on Caren's nerves and on the morale of her crew. Gruesome deaths continued to be reported at odd intervals. There seemed to be no pattern to either their timing or their location on the ship. Everyone was on edge. Not knowing when the person next to you — or you, yourself — might explode was a unique and terrifying experience.

Caren left Lieutenant Perkins in command and made her way to the research lab. She needed answers, and she needed them now. As she strode through the white and chrome corridors, doing her best to exude an air of confident authority, she acknowledged every crew member she passed, whether by name or with a brief nod of the head.

The manner of greeting was irrelevant. The important part was for the crew to see her as in control and moving purposefully. They were understandably rattled by recent events and needed to see their commanding officer behaving in a calm and competent manner. Needed to feel that the situation was being dealt with.

She only hoped that the physicist had actually found the answer. That the *hexaquarks* were indeed the guilty particles.

The doors to the research sector *whooshed* open. The pallid young man she'd spoken to on her viewscreen scrambled to greet her.

"Captain Fielding," he said. "It's an honor to meet you. I'm Research Assistant Second Class Rolf Markham. If you'll follow me, I'll take you to Dr. Okeke."

"Thank you, Markham."

The young man led her through a maze of sterile white counters covered in complex chrome and plasteel equipment. Machines hummed, clicked, and whirred, while white-coated staff spoke in low voices, sometimes into recorders, sometimes to each other. The air smelled of disinfectants, triggering Caren's memory of the too clean bridge and causing bile to rise in her throat. She coughed and choked it back down.

In addition to the white coats, many of the scientists wore safety goggles or face-plated helmets which obscured their features. Her guide stopped behind just such a pair and cleared his throat.

"Dr. Okeke, Dr. Inarsson," he said. "I'm sorry to disturb you, but Captain Fielding is here to see you."

Dr. Okeke turned, but the man, Dr. Inarsson, continued to stare into the viewscreen on the device he held. He straightened, his posture suddenly rigid. Without looking up, he bellowed, "Down! Everyone down!"

Caren dropped to the deck, her training too instinctual to allow for questions, But Markham remained upright. She grabbed for the cuff of his pants to encourage his compliance when his body crumpled. Warm liquid sprayed her face and hands and she closed her eyes. She knew without looking that the young man would never grow old.

The room was silent except for the mechanical sounds of the

still working machinery and a steady *drip ... drip ... drip* that Caren didn't want to think about. After what seemed an eternity, Dr. Inarsson called, "All clear!"

As she rose to her feet, Caren noticed that Dr. Okeke and Dr. Inarsson had remained on their feet. Both looked shaken. Dr. Okeke's normally glowing dark cocoa complexion had an ashen tinge, and even Dr. Inarsson's lips were white, but both scientists gazed at the containment canister held between them with an expression of barely suppressed awe.

Dr. Okeke turned to Caren and said quietly, "Dr. Inarsson managed to cobble together a functioning hexaquark detector. That's how he was able to see the particles enter the lab."

The tall blond scientist nodded. "The *hexaquarks* came through on a plane approximately three feet above the deck. That's why I called for everyone to get down. If all life forms were prone, they would be safe." He glanced at Markham's body. "I wish I'd had more time to explain."

"I'm grateful for the warning," Caren said, "And grateful to my early drill sergeants for beating that automatic response into me." She too glanced at Markham's remains, and, accepting a towel from a silent scientist, scrubbed his blood from her hands. "I guess we can now conclude that the *hexaquarks* are the cause of our recent spate of unexplained deaths."

Dr. Okeke nodded. "Yes, though I would have preferred a controlled experiment with a nonhuman subject."

"Agreed. May I ask why neither of you hit the floor," Caren asked, "and what that is that you're holding?"

"I could see their trajectories," Dr. Inarsson explained.

"And this canister holds a containment field that we hoped would capture a *hexaquark* for us to experiment with," Dr. Okeke continued. "Lars, Dr. Inarsson, built it at the same time as the detector."

Lars Inarrson was a tall, rangy man who appeared to be built entirely of angles. Sharp cheekbones, nose and chin. Long thin fingers that looked like they could substitute for scalpels. But the shy smile he wore now softened his angular appearance, allowing Caren to see the child he'd once been.

"It worked," he said quietly, his voice full of wonder. He met Caren's gaze "It was worth the risk, because it worked."

Caren glanced again at what had been Markham. His death brought the body count to twelve, maybe more — Perkins would update her when all decks had reported in — but at least now they knew the cause. Now they had a chance.

"Well done, doctors. I know it's early — you've just captured that particle — but do you have a recommendation?"

Dr. Okeke closed her eyes and drew a deep breath. Her shoulders slumped slightly, but her face regained a bit of its color. When she opened her eyes, she met Caren's gaze without hesitation. "I suggest we move as far as possible from the neutron star that is emitting the *hexaquarks*."

Caren nodded, but remained still, silently encouraging the doctor to continue.

When Dr. Okeke failed to speak, Dr. Inarsson picked up the narrative. "The particles travel in a straight line and, with no friction to interfere with their initial velocity, could continue to infinity. But the further we are from their source, the more distance there will be between their lines of travel. We should be able to reach a point where we can hide in the interstices between them." He met Caren's gaze. "Does that make sense?"

"It does," Caren replied. "Can you supply our navigation team with a detector so we'll know when we've reached a place of safety?"

Dr. Inarrson nodded. "I'll work with engineering to get a prototype wired into the navigational system."

"Very well. Let engineering know that this is a priority. I want this ship moved to safety as quickly as possible."

"Yes, sir," Dr. Inarsson said. "We'll continue our investigations with the contained *hexaquark* once we've reached a position of safety." He paused, then added, "Of presumed safety."

Caren nodded. "Understood. We have no guarantees at this point, but it's good to have a course of action."

4

Once *Odyssey* reached the coordinates Dr. Inarsson's detection device specified, Caren breathed a sigh of relief. Her crew should now be safe while the research sector carried out its investigation. She needed a solution. Something to make *Odyssey,* and every other ship in the fleet, *hexaquark-*proof.

Caren moved to the captain's chair and allowed it to enfold her. She turned to her communications officer and said, "Ensign Schaeffer, open a ship-wide channel."

"Aye, Captain," he said. "Channel open."

"Attention. This is Captain Fielding with an update on our current situation. *Odyssey's* research department has determined the cause of the recent deaths. We encountered uncategorized emissions from a neutron star. *Odyssey* has been bombarded by particles that have been theorized, but never before observed. Unfortunately, these particles are not compatible with human life."

She paused, composing her thoughts. "Fortunately, we have an excellent research team. Dr. Lars Inarsson has been able to build a detection device and we have moved to what we believe is a safe location. Dr. Inarsson and Dr. Chi Okeke have captured and contained a particle for study and are working with the research scientists to develop some form of protection against further incursion from these particles."

Caren glanced around the bridge and was relieved to see her bridge crew's expressions relaxing. The unknown had become known. Now it was just a matter of figuring out a fix. They could deal with that. They were good at that. They had confidence in the abilities of every member of *Odyssey's* crew. Now it was just a matter of time ... and hard work.

"I want to commend every member of this crew for your excellent work ethic under stressful conditions. Well done. Captain Fielding out."

She nodded to Ensign Schaeffer, who cut the transmission.

"Lt. Perkins," she said, catching her first officer's eye. "You have the conn. I'll be in my ready room. USL Command needs an update on our situation."

"Aye, sir."

Two days later, Caren again joined Dr. Okeke and Dr. Inarsson in *Odyssey's* research sector. The room remained bright, with light reflecting off the white walls and chrome work surfaces. It still smelled of disinfectant, but this time Caren's mind was calm, more removed from the gruesome deaths that had haunted her last visit. Machines still whirred and clicked and researchers still filled the air with a murmured buzz of conversation, but this time the atmosphere was less tense, the tang of fear was gone.

Dr. Inarsson greeted her at the door. "Captain Fielding. Thank you for coming."

Dr. Okeke moved to join them, once again exuding a calm, capable aura, though her eyes shone with excitement. "Come, sir. We have so much to show you."

The trio moved deeper into the white and chrome labyrinth, finally stopping before a small, glass-encased room.

"We've been running tests round the clock since we captured the *hexaquark*," Dr. Okeke said.

Dr. Inarsson nodded. "Our people have been very engaged. Young Markham was somewhat of a pet. His death touched us all. Brought the real world crashing through our scientific detachment."

"I can appreciate that," Caren said. "It's one thing to know people are dying. It's something else entirely to witness the event ... to be splattered with their blood."

"Yes," agreed Dr. Okeke. "We would've worked diligently regardless, but Markham's death provided a singular focus that has allowed us to move more quickly, with perhaps greater leaps of intuition."

"And what have you discovered?"

The two physicists exchanged a glance. Dr. Inarsson raised an eyebrow, and Dr. Okeke nodded.

"First," Dr. Inarsson began, gesturing toward the enclosed space, "the *hexaquark* remains contained. That is our best news. The field I initially developed and which allowed us to capture the particle has remained stable. The less satisfactory news is that the *hexaquark* passes through every other material we've put it in contact with as though the material didn't exist. Plastisteel, gold, silver, chrome, every material we've managed to get our hands on. Nothing stops it."

"Of course," Dr. Okeke said, "nothing is damaged by it either. It's as though the particle doesn't exist. Which is why we've seen no damage to the ship itself. Only the crew."

"Yes," continued Dr. Inarsson, "the particle has no effect on inanimate objects, no matter their composition. But life forms ... life is another matter entirely."

Dr. Okeke's eyes shone and her hands moved quickly across a virtual keyboard, bringing up a viewscreen with dozens of charts and diagrams. "It doesn't matter what type of life we expose to the particle: a seedling, an insect, even a microscopic bacterium; when a living organism comes in contact with the particle, it..." she moved her fisted hands apart and splayed her fingers, "explodes."

"More study will be required," Dr. Inarsson added, "to determine exactly what the catalyst is, for of course both animate and inanimate objects are ultimately made up of the same atomic particles, but for now, we have our answer."

"And that is?" asked Caren.

The scientists exchanged surprised glances. Evidently they thought they'd already explained it all.

"Why, that the particle is inimical to life," said Dr. Okeke.

"And that we'll need to work with engineering to add the containment field to our shields," said Dr. Inarsson. "But we'll need to reverse the polarity," he glanced at Dr. Okeke, who nodded, "in order to repel the particles rather than capturing them and adhering them to our hull."

"I see," Caren said, and she did. At least the part about repelling instead of adhering. "Let me know when we have a workable shield. Until then, since we've suffered no new deaths, we'll remain where we are."

She stared at the diagrams and charts still displayed on the viewscreen and shook her head. She'd been called something of a tactical genius, but this information left her feeling like a school girl again. Thank the universe (and the fleet and academy she represented) she had a full complement of scientists aboard. She'd have had no idea how to proceed without them.

"Well done, doctors. Between you and the engineers, we'll be able to ensure that no other USL ship ever has to experience the trauma we've endured these last few days."

"Thank you, sir," said Dr. Inarsson.

"We'll let you know as soon as we have a workable shield," Dr. Okeke said.

Caren nodded, and with a *whoosh* of the door, left the scientists to their work.

Returning to her ready room, she collapsed into the tawny faux leather of her padded desk chair and, closing her eyes, allowed herself to mourn. The crisis was past. The *incident* had been explained. Now, at last, she could allow herself to acknowledge her loss.

Blake was dead.

His death had left a whole in the fabric of her life that might never be fully repaired, but she had not fallen apart. She had seen it through, as he would have wanted ... as he would have expected. The cost had been high, fifteen lives had been lost all told, but *Odyssey's* duty as an exploratory vessel had been fulfilled. An Old Earth theory had been confirmed; a new particle had been catalogued, its properties recorded. Human knowledge and experience had been expanded.

And, yes, life went on.

COPYRIGHT

INCIDENT ON THE ODYSSEY
Copyright © 2019 by Debbie Mumford
Published by WDM Publishing
Cover and Layout copyright © 2019 by WDM Publishing
Cover design by WDM Publishing
Cover art copyright © Veronika Surovtseva | Dreamstime.com

REMEMBRANCE

1

WHAT WAS

$\mathcal{I}$ am a child of the Cold War. When I imagined humanity's annihilation, I envisioned sinister mushroom clouds blighting the world's landscapes, their deadly concussive waves roiling across the earth like tsunamis of destruction.

But Mother Earth is more subtle than man. The death she sent was imperceptible, so quiet we didn't even realize we'd been struck a fatal blow.

I am dying, as all men must, as humanity itself now will. I have no regrets. I have lived a full life; born healthy children; seen them grow to adulthood; held my grandchildren in my arms. No, my regrets are not for things left undone in my life, but for the generations that will not come after me.

I am surrounded by the familiar: the bed I shared with my beloved husband for nearly seventy years supports me in my decline, the quilt I made for his fortieth birthday comforts me, its colors still jewel bright though my sight is dimming. The room is lit by the soft glow of candles in jars, a whim of my youngest daughter. She hopes the sweet aromas of lavender, jasmine, and chamomile will tempt my soul to stay, but I am not interested in lingering. I know what the future holds and I am ready to relinquish my place in it.

I study the faces of my family. The legacy my beloved and I created together in love. Strong, handsome sons. Beautiful, capable daughters. And the grandchildren, grown to adulthood now, though I will always remember them as infants.

There should be great-grandchildren as well. That is my sorrow. The loss of the precious lives that might have been.

My daughters have known the joys and fears of motherhood; my granddaughters never will. I mourn for the birthright they will never experience.

The exquisite pain of childbirth: sheer physical labor that saps the strength and leaves you panting and begging for relief. The inexpressible joy when it is finished and the soft, warm weight you have carried so long beneath your heart is finally placed in your arms. The wonder of seeing your child's features for the first time: your button nose, his cleft chin, the shape of your mother's ear. Ten tiny fingers clutching your one. Toes curling as delicately as rose petals. Tufts of downy-soft hair and skin so smooth and silky you're afraid your rough fingers will mar its perfection.

And the smell! The glorious, delicious smell of infancy, an indescribable but unmistakable combination of warm skin, soft breath, milk, and primal magic that binds a mother to her child, making it nearly impossible to put your newborn down or allow someone else to take the babe from your arms.

This is what we have lost. This is what will never come again.

I glance at each beloved face and my gaze comes to rest on my youngest granddaughter. Her life will be so very different from mine. She may very well live to see the end of our race. She lifts her eyes and meets my gaze. We mourn for each other.

I close my eyes. My time has come.

2

WHAT WILL BE

*G*randmama closes her eyes and passes from this life with a sigh. I know she worried about us, about me. I felt it in her final glance. My life will not be what she and my parents hoped for me, but it is the only life I have. The only one I have ever known.

Grandmama mourned that I would never have children, that I might live to see the end of our species, that I might be alone in the world at the end.

But she was wrong. The life I will lead, am leading, was unfathomable to her as it is incomprehensible to my parents. I have joined a group of my fellow end-timers — those of us born in the last year that humanity birthed children — and we are laboring to bring another form of life into existence.

My parents' generation used to speculate on the possibility of a man-machine amalgam known as the singularity. They expected it to be a naturally occurring mutation. Unfortunately, Mother Nature took us down a different, completely unexpected path.

But now my friends and I are working diligently to bring that possibility to fruition.

We don't delude ourselves that our creation will save mankind, but we do hope that our brain-child will preserve a record of our existence, will bear witness to any other intelligent species who might someday discover our planet that once our species lived and dreamed and believed ourselves invincible.

This creation, this artificial intelligence, this brain-child will be my legacy. The legacy of all mankind. This is the final pregnancy we labor to bring to term before my generation joins Grandmama in oblivion and the final nights falls on our species.

I pay my last respects to Grandmama, hug Mother, her youngest daughter, and quietly leave the rest of my family to grieve. I have work to do and only my short life-span to accomplish the task.

I join my team at our laboratory. As more and more people die of natural causes — or take their own lives in despair — work space and equipment become more readily available. Grandmama's generation is nearly gone, Mother and Dad's generation has lost heart. They no longer see the point of climbing corporate ladders or struggling to excel in their chosen careers. Even the artists of their generation have lost their focus. Why create when in a few short years there will be no one to view, read, or listen to their efforts?

My generation is, on the whole, manic. Hedonism has reached new heights. Live for the moment and the pleasure it can bring! Why work or behave in a socially acceptable manner? Our elders have no relevance. They will soon be dead. Yes, we can live full life-spans, but why bother? When we die, it's all over anyway, so why not simply live to experience everything now?

Fatal accidents are rampant. There's no reason not to risk life itself. Death is inevitable and there is no future to plan and work for. What does it matter if we die today, tomorrow, next month, or fifty years from now? The end will still be the end.

My team and I are lucky that so many systems are now automated. Basic utilities will outlive our species. Food is becoming less varied as transportation and distribution systems break down, but several of our group have family farms and parents and siblings willing to support our work with their efforts. Our needs are met, and those who meet them are rewarded with a sense of purpose. Something that has all but disappeared.

We are a world unto ourselves. Our small team of computer experts, mechanical engineers, historians, philosophers, and dreamers. We design, build, program, test. We discover bugs, run up against seemingly insurmountable issues, curse fate and the slowness of technological advances, and return to the design board.

Years pass. Attrition dwindles our family. Mom calls to tell me my cousin, a boy just a year older than me, has died from alcohol poisoning. A dare from a friend. They died within hours of each other. I wonder who won the dare, or whether their final idiocy was a draw?

I express my condolences to my aunt and uncle and return to the laboratory.

The work continues. We celebrate a breakthrough. The latest cerebral interface looks promising. All of the initial tests are positive. What is needed now is a human subject.

I volunteer.

When I visit my family for the final time, Mother and Dad are bemused. They never expected to outlive their only child. Of course, they never expected their world to end, either.

I explain that if the experiment works, I will never die.

Yes, my body will cease to function and decay, but my mind will join the artificial intelligence we have created. I will become one with Omega and my thoughts and memories will live on. Omega will remember Grandmama and everything she ever told me about the joys of motherhood, the precious moments of infancy, the complete captivation that a mother feels for her newborn.

Mother and Dad shake their heads, but hug me and send me forward with their blessing and their fervent hope that these dreams of mine come true.

I walk into the lab on my last day as a human being. My team opens a bottle of champagne and we drink a toast to our success, to my continued awareness.

I step up to the padded lounge, rather like the chair my dentist used to have me sit in before cavities became too trivial to be of concern, and my best friend settles the cerebral interface on my head. I feel like I've been crowned empress of the world.

I smile at each of my team members, as Grandmama smiled at each of her family members before she breathed her last, and I close my eyes.

Jared counts backward from ten.

My last conscious thought is of this final infant which we have labored to bring into existence ...

Omega.

COPYRIGHT

SELKIES IN PARADISE

PROLOGUE

*M*y name is Artie Woodward-Kendrick, and I'm the luckiest woman in the world. I'm married to my very best friend, Jed Kendrick.

Who could've guessed I'd ever find someone to love; that I would ever marry? Certainly not me!

You see, I'm a seer. I see things normal people don't, things they couldn't see, even if they wanted to ... which no one in their right mind would. I mean let's get real; even I don't want to see the Fae. But I don't have a choice. I was born with this strange ability to see the unseen, to know the unknowable.

I thought I was alone. Thought I'd be alone my entire life. I knew I'd never find love.

Sure, my mom and dad loved me, but even they thought I was weird. They worried about me constantly when I was a kid, dragged me to more shrinks than I care to remember. None of them helped. After all, everyone assumed I was imagining things.

Only I wasn't.

So I learned to hide.

By the time I made it to high school, I was adept at hiding. I hid my knowledge from my parents. I tried desperately to hide my weirdness from the kids at school. But most importantly, I hid the fact that I could see what I'd named *the terrors*, that I knew they existed, from the terrors themselves. And as long as I hid, I was safe.

Lonely ... but safe.

So how did I manage to find a man who not only befriended me, but who grew to love me? How did my life change from hidden and lonely to fulfilled and glowing with contentment?

Jed Kendrick moved to my hometown in Colorado.

We recognized each other, and our loneliness ended. We were both seers, and on our first day at McKinley High we became a team, but that's another story. Suffice it to say that over the last six and a half years we've fought terrors and other forms of Fae from Colorado to Ireland.

And somewhere along the way, we fell in love.

Now, I'm glowing with happiness because just a few days ago, on a glorious late November day — Thanksgiving Day to be exact — I became Jed Kendrick's wife, and he became Artie Woodward's husband. The Woodward-Kendrick team became official in the eyes of the world.

What's next, you ask? Who knows! But whatever it is, we'll face it together.

Right after we get home from the awesome honeymoon our family and friends arranged for us ... in Hawaii!

1

On a crystal clear day in late November, our plane landed in paradise. Aside from a fateful trip to Ireland to meet Jed's Grannie O'Toole, I'd never been beyond the borders of Colorado, so when I stepped from the plane into the open-air terminal at Lihui Airport on the Hawaiian island of Kauai, I was overwhelmed. I stopped in the midst of a throng of people, clinging to Jed's arm, and inhaled the exotic mixture of sea salt, tropical flowers, and lushly green growing things.

Jed squeezed my hand and smiled down at me. "We're here," he said, his voice tinged with amazement. "We're actually married and on our honeymoon."

I nodded, momentarily lost in the love and wonder shining in his eyes. There had been moments in Ireland when I'd despaired of ever seeing Jed's handsome face again, and now here we were … married and on the island of Kauai.

Before I could answer, a pretty young woman with a water-fall of shining black hair and sun-kissed skin stepped up to us. She wore a sleeveless red dress patterned with huge white flowers, and her arms dripped with brightly colored flower leis.

"Aloha," she said as she placed a lei around each of our necks. "Welcome to Kauai. We hope you'll enjoy your stay."

I smiled my thanks, but my attention was caught by the beauty of the flowers that made up my lei. I'd never seen, or smelled, anything like them. I recognized white carnations in the necklace of flowers, but the other varieties were a mystery.

I glanced up and met her gaze. "Thank you. These are beautiful, but what kind of flowers are they?"

She held up another of the leis she carried and indicated a white, star-like flower edged in delicate pink. "This is plumeria. Most of the fragrance of your lei comes from it. You'll see them often here in the islands. Sometimes in pink, often in yellow." Pointing to other flowers in turn she said, "We also use tuberoses, carnations, orchids, and jasmine, but you'll see many other types of leis during your stay." She smiled again, and with a little wave, turned to greet another couple.

Jed fingered the lei around his neck — his was made up of darker, more bold colors than mine and featured quite a bit of greenery — and said, "Wow. I didn't expect to be given flowers just for walking off a plane."

"They look good on you," I said, grinning up at my tall, lanky husband. I'd nearly lost Jed in Ireland. He'd been ensorcelled and held thrall by the Fae, and I'd almost given up hope of finding a way to rescue him. But Grannie O'Toole and Laird Angus had helped me and ... well, that was a tale I didn't want to think about right now.

It was enough to have him here with me, to be able to watch him examine his lei while I admired his more-than-six-foot frame, his tousled black hair, and his gentle gray eyes rimmed by long and lovely dark lashes. His full lips twitched as he noticed my stare.

"Like what you see?" he asked, his eye color darkening to a smoldering, smoky gray.

"Always," I replied, my heart beating faster as memories of our wedding night crowded my mind. "Let's find our luggage."

"Yes," he agreed, licking his lips. "I think we need to check out our accommodations." He swallowed, his Adam's apple bobbing. "Soon."

2

Our hotel suite was stunning. The laird had gone all out for us after our Irish misadventure. He'd booked us into a luxury resort on Kauai's north shore and made sure we had all the amenities. I wandered through the sitting room and stepped through the sliding glass door onto the ocean-view lanai, while Jed tipped the young man who'd brought our luggage up.

A soft murmur of voices, the muffled thump of a closing door, and a moment later Jed was beside me, his arms sliding around my waist. We gazed at the picture postcard view of palm trees, white sand and impossibly blue water and then turned to each other.

"Welcome to paradise," Jed murmured as he drew me close and bent to kiss me.

His lips were soft and warm, and I melted into his embrace. Jed loved me. He understood me. He was my partner in life, my equal. And now ... right now, he was my lover.

Our kiss deepened, became more passionate, and when the spark it kindled grew to a flame, he pulled away. The light in his eyes echoed the smoldering heat growing in my core. In one quick movement, he bent and, moving one strong arm behind my knees, swept me off my feet and into his arms. Without a word, my lover carried me across the sitting room and into the bedroom ... to the perfectly arranged and very enticing king-size bed.

"You're wearing too many clothes," he whispered as he placed me gently on the pillow-soft mattress.

"So are you," I answered in voice so husky I barely recognized it as my own.

We remedied that little problem and spent the next few hours doing what newlyweds have done since time immemorial: exploring each other's bodies and discovering new depths of our love.

Our first day on Kauai was drawing to a close when we emerged from our hotel suite in search of food. We opted for dinner on the terrace overlooking Hanalei Bay. I watched the sun sink into the darkening water, marveling at the vivid shades of red and gold as I savored firm, sweet flakes of mahi mahi flavored with mango sauce and delicious coconut rice.

Jed caught my free hand in his, stroking my fingers with his thumb. We didn't speak. No words were needed. We simply drank in the moment, appreciating the tranquility and peace of this beautiful place.

After dinner, we wandered through the open air hotel lobby and down a stone-paved path to a pristine white sand beach. The rolling waves of the bay beckoned us with their froth of white lace.

We strolled hand-in-hand in the moonlight, serenaded by the susurrus of water on sand, cooled by a light sea breeze that lifted my long dark hair and ruffled Jed's black locks. As we rounded the curve of the bay, I noticed a woman in a long white dress sitting in the sand at the edge of the water. Her knees were pulled up so that her chin rested on them, the gentle waves kissing her feet with each inward flow. We walked a few steps closer, and she raised her head and glanced at us. Moonlight shimmered on her face, and I saw that it was glazed with tears.

I laid my free hand on Jed's arm to stop him, disentangled my fingers from his, and stepped nearer to the woman. Closer now, I saw that she was young, not much older than me, with lovely dark slanting eyes. But the moonlight played tricks with her hair, making the nearly waist-length sable waves appear to have a silvery sheen.

"Are you hurt?" I asked, just loudly enough to be heard over the waves. "Can we help you?"

And then Jed was beside me, pulling me back toward the resort. "Come away from her, Artie," he whispered urgently in my ear. "Can't you see what she is?"

I looked again, and saw what my love had seen.

The young woman had risen. She stood with her feet in a froth of water, her long white dress wet to the knees, one hand held out to us in a gesture of supplication. An unearthly glow surrounded her, one not detectable by normal human eyes ... but neither Jed nor I were normal humans. We were seers. And right now our sight showed us a woman of the Fae.

"Please," she said, making no move to approach us. "Please, can you help me?"

Jed pushed me behind him, but made no move to flee. "What could a mortal do to help a Fae woman?"

She gasped and stumbled back a step. "Y-you know what I am?"

I stepped to Jed's side, despite his annoyed glance. "Not precisely," I said. "Only that you aren't human."

Nodding, she moved closer, hesitantly, like a wild animal. Curious, but cautious. And always with her feet in the waves.

"I'm a selkie," she said, her dark eyes wide and full of pain, "but I can't return home to the sea. Someone has stolen my skin. I'm marooned here, with no one to tell my kin what has become of me. Can you help me? Can you at least carry a message to my colony?"

A selkie. One of that ancient race of shape-shifters who live in the oceans of the world, appearing to human eyes as seals in the water, and transforming into human form on land. But the transformation required a catalyst. To become human, a selkie had to shed its skin, which was then carefully hidden. Very carefully, because without its skin, the creature was powerless to shift into its true form and return to the water.

"We've learned to distrust the Fae," Jed said, his voice low and menacing. "My wife may be sympathetic, but I won't risk her on what could be a trick."

Tears streamed across her cheeks as she shook her head. "It's no trick. I'm desperate, and you're the only ones who can possibly understand my plight. Please, help me." She wiped her cheeks with trembling hands, took a deep breath, and continued. "If you won't seek out my kin, at least tell Maris where I am and what has happened."

"Who?" Jed and I asked simultaneously.

"Maris Grainger," said the selkie woman. "She lives on Maui. I have no money and I can no longer swim, so I can't reach her. Go to Maui, to Maalaea Harbor. Look for Captain Bill's Island Cruises. Her father works there. He'll tell you how to find Maris. Tell her Serena needs her help. She'll go to my family. Maris will know what to do."

I frowned. "Is she a seer?" I asked, confused. "How can this Maris Grainger help you?"

"Maris is special," she said. "Different. Neither Fae nor human, but she's kind and cares for all who inhabit the sea.

She'll help. She'll know what to do. Please, tell Maris Serena needs her."

Jed and I exchanged a glance. We'd planned to do some sight-seeing on Maui anyway, and an island cruise sounded lovely. I quirked an eyebrow at him and he shrugged his shoulders in a *might as well* kind of way. I grinned and stood on tiptoe to kiss his cheek.

"We'll see if we can find Maris tomorrow," I said.

The selkie nodded. "Thank you."

Jed and I turned and practically ran back to the resort.

"Well, that's a first," Jed said quietly when we were safely back in the open air lobby. "A member of the Fae asking for our help."

I nodded. Every other encounter we'd ever had with that race of supernatural creatures had been hostile. As we took the elevator to our suite, I wondered what manner of being this Maris Grainger might be. Not Fae. Not human. Then what exactly was she?

Evidently a being who was kind and cared for sea creatures.

How intriguing!

3

The next morning we caught an island hopper flight to Kapalua Airport on Maui, rented a red Jeep Wrangler, and drove to Maalaea Harbor. What a wonderfully adventurous start to our day! Flying over the emerald jewel of Kauai and the diamond-tipped sapphire of the Pacific before landing on Maui's northwest coast. We drove south along Highway 30, the open-topped Wrangler giving us clear views of the ocean to the west and the stunning West Maui Mountains to the east.

We arrived in Maalaea Town a little before noon and went in search of Captain Bill's Island Cruises. The young woman manning the ticket booth told us that the Graingers sailed on the Sea Princess, which was currently on a whale watching run, but that we could book seats on the Sea Princess for its 2:00 p.m. snorkeling cruise.

Jed pulled out the credit card Laird Angus had provided and paid for our afternoon adventure. The young woman advised us to be back by 1:30 to board the Sea Princess and grab choice seats.

Pushing his wallet back into his pocket, Jed turned to me.

"Shall we find some lunch? We've got a little over an hour to kill."

As if on cue, my stomach growled, loudly.

"I'll take that as a 'yes,'" Jed said with a laugh, and we turned and strolled across the street and down a block to King Kamehameha's Crab Shack. Snagging a table on the patio overlooking the bay, we studied the menu, a large chalk board hung above the serving window.

"I think I'll try the crab cakes," I said, mouth watering in anticipation.

"Yeah, those look good," Jed answered, eyeing another patron's plate briefly before looking back to the menu, "but I'm going for the coconut shrimp." He glanced at me, smiled, and said, "You sit still and enjoy the view. I'll go order."

The view was certainly worth savoring. The deep blue waters of Maalaea Bay; the dark outline of hills around the curve of beach; the neat masts of ships in their slips along the dock, as well as the full-bellied sails of those returning from their errands on the ocean's deep water. All covered by a sky so clear and blue it felt unreal. I'd always thought my little corner of Colorado enjoyed clear skies, but that was before I came to Hawaii.

Jed came back carrying plates loaded with delicious smelling food.

"Wow," I said, accepting my lunch. "That was fast."

He nodded, sat down, grabbed a piece of breaded shrimp and dragged it through a deep red sauce. "I didn't expect to be handed our plates as soon as I paid." He popped the shrimp into this mouth, chewed, swallowed, and grabbed another. "This is really good!"

I cut into my first crab cake with my fork, lifted it to my lips and sighed with contentment as the moist, flavorful tidbit hit my tongue. "Oh, yeah," I murmured between bites. "If we were staying on Maui, I could eat here every day."

We finished our meal, but lingered at the crab shack's table, sipping POG, a refreshing passion fruit-orange-guava juice drink, and alternately watching the bay and our fellow tourists. The number of people walking around in skimpy swimsuits and flip-flops made me feel positively overdressed in my khaki shorts and bright pink T-shirt. Of course, Jed and I both wore swimsuits too; we just wore regular clothes over them.

A little after 1:00 we saw the Sea Princess slip into place at Captain Bill's dock. Happy tourists disembarked, their necks slung with cameras, the afternoon sun glinting off sunglasses and binoculars.

Jed stood and held out a hand to me. "Shall we?"

"We shall," I answered with a grin. "I'm really anxious to meet this Maris person. I wonder how Serena expects the girl to help?"

"No clue. I just hope she's actually on the boat with her dad and not off having a picnic with friends or something."

I nodded. We'd made this trip to meet Maris Grainger, and one way or another, we would do so. If she wasn't aboard the Sea Princess, we'd just have to keep an eye on her father, Richard, until he led us to her.

We needn't have worried. When we boarded the Sea Princess, we were greeted by a teenage girl with short, curly red hair, dozens of freckles across her nose ... and a faint other-worldly glow outlining her trim young body. She was dressed much as I was, in neatly pressed khaki shorts and a T-shirt, but her T was emblazoned with Captain Bill's name and logo.

"Welcome aboard the Sea Princess," she said, taking our tickets and checking our names off on a clipboard. "Please find a seat. The mate will explain what we're about in a few minutes."

We walked on. No point it trying to talk to her now; she needed to get the rest of the passengers aboard.

Moving forward, we claimed seats along the bow rail of the little ship. A few minutes later a tall man wearing khaki trousers, a short-sleeved white shirt, and wrap-around sunglasses unhooked a microphone and called for our attention.

"Welcome aboard the Sea Princess," he announced. "I'm Richard Grainger, and I'll be your guide today. We'll be setting sail in a minute or two for Molokini Crater where you'll enjoy some of the best snorkeling in the islands. Our sailing time will be about an hour, so please pay attention while I give you some necessary safety information."

I listened to the man's speech, at least enough to take note of where the life preservers were stowed, but most of my attention was focused on Maris. True, we hadn't asked the teen's name, but normal human girls didn't have a glowing aura.

Frowning, I watched the girl as she moved quietly and confidently across the deck. Something was off. She definitely had a nimbus, but it wasn't as bright and clearly defined as that of most Fae. Hers was somehow softer, more misty than I'd come to expect.

Neither did I see the image of her true form upon her human body. When the Fae choose to be seen by mortal men, they wrap themselves in a glamour. They appear human, no matter what their true forms may be.

Because of our unique heritage, Jed and I see the Fae for what they really are. Our *sight* allows us to see past the image they project to their true selves. We see their human disguise superimposed upon their other-worldly forms.

Maris presented a soft Fae nimbus, but I saw no trace of another form.

"What is she?" I wondered quietly to Jed.

He shook his head and adjusted his sunglasses on his nose.

"I don't know," he answered, just as quietly, "but her father is pure human." He nodded toward our guide. "I wonder if he's really her father, or just some poor schmuck she's ensorcelled into believing they're related?"

"No telling, but we've got an hour to find out what's going on."

Richard Grainger had ended his spiel by inviting the passengers to explore the ship, enjoy non-alcoholic beverages and snacks in the lounge off the galley, and watch for passing humpback whales, which he promised to point out if any were spotted by the crew.

With forty or so passengers moving freely around the decks, we'd be able to approach Maris easily.

"Let me talk to her first," I said, laying a hand on Jed's arm. "We don't want to scare her by ganging up on her."

He nodded. "Okay, but stay in plain sight. We don't know what she's capable of."

I patted his arm. "Don't worry. I won't underestimate her."

Maris stood against the wall in the lounge, presumably keeping an eye on the platters of food in order to restock as needed. I picked up plate, arranged a slice of pineapple, some bits of cheese, and a couple of crackers on it, and then moved to stand beside her while I nibbled.

"This is a nice boat," I said, trying to sound casual. "Is it a yacht?"

The girl smiled and her nimbus glowed a bit brighter. "The Sea Princess is a double-hulled catamaran, a very stable yacht."

I wiped my fingers on a napkin and held out my hand. "I'm Artie," I said, and nodding toward Jed, added, "that's my husband, Jed. We're on our honeymoon." I grinned, blushing slightly.

Maris took my hand. Hers was warm, her handshake firm.

This close, I could see the ghostly image of long, slim fingers, webbed almost to the tips.

"I'm Maris Grainger," she said. "Congratulations."

"Thanks." I released her hand and, picking up a piece of cheese, nibbled a bite. "Grainger," I said, as though considering. "Are you related to the mate who's our guide?"

She dimpled. "He's my dad. We moved out here from Kansas about a year ago."

"Kansas? Really? And you're both working on a sailing ship? That seems a bit odd."

She shrugged. "Dad was a sailor before he met my mom. They lived in Hawaii for a while, but moved inland when I was a baby."

"How interesting!" I glanced around for more people in Captain Bill T's. "Is your mom on board too?"

Her smile disappeared, a deep sadness filling her eyes. "No. Mom died in a car accident in Kansas.

"Oh," I said quickly. "I'm so sorry."

We stood in silence for a few moments. I glanced at Jed, who met my gaze with solemn reassurance. He couldn't hear what Maris and I had said, but stood ready to assist if needed.

I took a deep breath and decided to take the plunge. The lounge held only a few people, no one near enough to hear what I said to her next.

"Maris," I said quietly, "Jed and I, well, we're what's known as *Seers*. We see things other people can't." She stiffened, and I placed a hand on her arm. "We can see that you're not, well, you're not exactly human."

She startled, tried to pull away. I tightened my grip on her arm.

"Please don't leave," I said, putting as much compassion in my voice as I could. "We mean you no harm, but we have a message for you."

She stilled. I knew she was ready to flee, but stood her ground, quietly wary. I dropped my restraining hand.

"What kind of message?"

"Do you mind if Jed joins us?" I asked. "We didn't want to scare you by both approaching you at once."

She glanced in his direction, moved a little to her left, giving herself a clear path to the door, and nodded. "All right. He can come over, and I'll listen, but if you try to hurt me, I'm screaming for Dad."

I beckoned to Jed as I said, "We're not interested in causing you any trouble, Maris. We just need to talk to you."

Jed strode across the room and stopped beside me. "You must be Maris," he said, holding out his hand and giving her his most charming smile. "I'm Jed Kendrick and I'm very glad to meet you."

She put her hand in his, a bit timidly, but managed a smile when he released her after a brief shake.

"I was just about to tell Maris about our encounter last night," I said.

"Great," he said. "Why don't we sit down at that table. We might as well be comfortable while we talk."

Once we were all seated, I told Maris our tale. "We're honeymooning on the north shore of Kauai, and last night while we were strolling along the beach, we met a young woman. Only she wasn't ... a woman, I mean. She was a selkie in human form." I paused and studied Maris's face. "Her name is Serena." Maris's eyes widened. She knew Serena.

"Someone stole her skin," I continued, "and she's stranded in human form. She told us about you. Asked us to find you and tell you that she needs help." I paused again, a frown tightening my brow. "The thing is, neither Jed nor I can imagine how you, a teenage girl, can possibly help her."

Maris exhaled the breath she'd been holding and said, "Oh!

That's terrible. I may not be able to help, but I can let her colony know where she is and what's happened to her. They may be able to figure out how to get her home. At least she'll be with her family again, even if she is cut off from the sea."

"Her colony?" I asked blankly.

The girl nodded. "She's a member of a colony of selkies that lives on Ni'ihau."

"The Forbidden Island?" Jed asked.

"That's right," Maris said, nodding. "It's a private island and most of it is uninhabited. It's a haven for Hawaiian Monk seals, and the selkies decided to make it their home as well. They're related to the Monk seals, after all."

"They are?" Jed and I said together.

"Sure. The Hawaiian selkies are descended from a few Scottish selkies who decided to try their luck with human sailing. When their ship was destroyed in a storm, they managed to grab their skins, transform, and swim to safety. They joined a herd of Hawaiian Monk seals and eventually interbred and became the selkies of Ni'ihau."

"Wow," I said. "I had no idea."

"And how do you fit into all of this?" Jed asked. "What exactly are you?"

Maris glanced around the lounge, but we were the only occupants at the moment. The loudspeaker had announced a whale sighting a few moments before and everyone but us had raced to the port rail to see.

"I'm a siren," she said. "Well, technically, I'm only half siren. My dad, as you probably noticed, is completely normal. Evidently my mom was a real siren."

She shrugged. "I'm a little fuzzy on the details 'cause I didn't know anything about it until last year. Mom kept me away from salt water because she didn't know if my blood would be strong enough to allow me to transform, but she knew I'd be drawn to the sea. So I grew up in Kansas."

"And she never told you?" Jed asked, a little callously in my opinion, but then he hadn't been there to see the look in Maris's eyes when she spoke of her mother's death.

"She died before she got around to explaining," Maris said.

Jed had the grace to look uncomfortable. "Sorry," he said quietly.

"But now I know," Maris continued, her tone brightening, "and Dad and I live here now and I get to swim in the ocean with my friends every day."

"So, do you snorkel with the tourists?" I asked.

"No. I stay on the Sea Princess while everyone snorkels." She grinned. "Wouldn't want to scare away the tourists."

"Of course," Jed said with a nod. "You wouldn't need any equipment, and you probably change shape."

She nodded. "Not as much as a selkie, but it's noticeable. I can swim with my dad, but no one else. At least not in salt water. In fresh water, I stay human."

"Fascinating." I said, and Jed nodded his agreement.

Snorkeling at Molokini Crater was wonderful. The turquoise waters were crystal clear, with no sediment to impede our vision. We marveled at the many types of colorful tropical fish as they darted around us, and thrilled to the stately sea turtles that swam so close we could almost touch them. I was truly disappointed when it was time to board the Sea Princess and return to port. But Maris met us with towels and promised to introduce us to a pod of dolphins before we left, so I was content to act the compliant tourist.

As we drove the Jeep back to Kapalua Airport, Jed and I

agreed we'd had a very successful day. We'd done the tourist thing, had a taste of snorkeling in paradise, and had fulfilled our promise to Serena. Best of all, Maris had promised to meet us the next afternoon at Hanalei Bay, where we hoped to give the selkie good news.

It was nice to know that not all Fae were evil creatures. Far from needing to protect humanity from selkies, it seemed that, in Hawaii at least, selkies needed protection from humans!

4

The next afternoon we strolled the white sand of Hanalei Bay again, only this time we had to thread our way past beach umbrellas and relaxed people resting on towels soaking up the bright Hawaiian sunshine. Swimsuit clad humans frolicked in the gentle waves, while the more adventurous could be seen adjusting their masks and fins before plunging beneath the surface of the salt water.

Jed and I meandered around the curve of the bay to a rocky outcropping where a lone figure sat staring out to sea, her dark hair billowing in the breeze.

"May we join you?" I asked Serena when we were close enough to speak comfortably above the susurrus of waves and wind.

She glanced up and nodded, a small, sad smile gracing her lovely features. "Of course. It's good to see you again."

I settled on a flattish rock beside her while Jed squatted at my other side. "We found Maris," he said, shading his eyes and glancing out to sea.

Serena sat a little straighter and stared at him, hope shining in her eyes. "What did she say? Will she help?"

I nodded, answering before Jed had the chance. "She said she'd meet us here this afternoon. I don't know when exactly, but…"

"There!" cried Jed, pointing at the water. "I think she's coming. That swimmer is too far out to be a tourist."

Serena and I both gazed in the direction he pointed, and after a moment's searching, I saw something bobbing in the water. Something that came closer and became more distinct as I watched.

"It's her," Serena said, excitement ringing in her voice, "and look! She's not alone. She's brought one of my colony."

A few moments later — faster than I would've thought possible — Maris emerged from the sea, like a red-haired, bikini-clad goddess. She was followed by a seal, who dipped beneath the surface and emerged again as a man with dark hair graying at the temples.

If I hadn't been watching closely, I wouldn't have noticed the unnatural elongation of Maris' hands and feet, or the webbing between her fingers and toes. Her transformation back to human-appearing teen was nearly instantaneous.

The man who followed her onto the rocky outcrop carried what looked like a wet ball of fur, held strategically since he wore no clothes. He didn't seem at all embarrassed by his state of undress. In fact, I had the impression that he held what was undoubtedly his seal skin in that precise location for my benefit alone.

Jed and I rose to our feet as Maris and the selkie approached. Serena jumped to her feet and ran to the man. He dropped his skin and enveloped her in a hug.

"Serena," he said. "We've been so worried. I'm relieved to find you whole and well."

"Father," she said with a sob. "I'm stranded. I can't come home!"

I glanced away from the selkies, feeling that I intruded on their reunion. I turned my attention to Maris instead, and saw that she too carried a wet ball of fur. Puzzled, I glanced back at the father and daughter. No, the man's skin lay at his feet, where he had dropped it to embrace his daughter.

Turning back to Maris, I quirked an eyebrow and nodded to the skin in her hands. But before she could answer my unspoken question, the seal-man cleared his throat.

"The Selkies of Niʻihau are in your debt, Seers," he said with a formality that rang with Fae magic. The Fae rarely acknowledged obligation to humans, but when they did, it carried a binding geas. Jed reached for my hand, and we held tight to each other.

"We thought our daughter lost forever, but the message you carried has restored her to us." He inclined his head to us, his dark eyes shining with sincerity. "We acknowledge our debt. Word will be sent from dolphin to whale to seal until every one of our kind in the world knows of your deed. If ever you are in need and a selkie is near, we will render what assistance we can." He paused to stare directly into Jed's eyes and then my own. "Selkies do not forget. Never would we have expected such a kindness from a seer. You are unique ... and we will remember."

Chills ran down my spine despite the sun's heat. I knew I should respond, but no words came. My mind felt frozen by the selkie's words.

Fortunately, my husband has always been the socially adept member of our team.

"We acknowledge your gift," he said solemnly, "though we don't feel its need. What we did was a small thing. Carrying your daughter's message cost us little and gained us knowledge, not only of your kind, but of Maris as well. We value such knowledge. Let us part as friends ... with no debt between us."

I squeezed Jed's fingers in appreciation of his words.

The selkie studied us for a long moment. "You are gracious, Seer. We release the obligation of indebtedness in favor of friendship. May the Selkies of Niʻihau and the members of your bloodline remember this day to eternity. Let there be friendship between our people."

He inclined his head to us, and Jed and I responded in kind.

"And now," he said, turning to his daughter, "we must get you home."

Serena sobbed and tears streamed down her cheeks. "But how? My skin is lost!"

Maris stepped forward, speaking for the first time. "Your mother sent you her skin," she said, holding out the dripping fur. "Wear it for your journey home."

Serena's eyes widened as she accepted the skin, stroking it wistfully. "Is this possible, Father?"

He nodded. "Only from a close relative can such a sacrifice be made, and only in extremis, but yes, you may wear your mother's skin for this journey."

He turned back to me and Jed. "We will take our leave now, Seers. Know that our offer of future assistance holds." He held up a hand when Jed started to object. "Not out of debt or obligation, but out of friendship. Farewell, Seers-Who-Are-Friends-of-Selkies. May your lives be rich and fruitful."

"Farewell, Selkies of Niʻihau," Jed responded. "May that which is lost be found."

And with that, Serena and her father slipped into the water, donned their skins, and swam swiftly into the depths of the blue Pacific.

EPILOGUE

*J*ed and I had been home from our Hawaiian honeymoon for less than a month when we received a letter from Maris. I opened it quickly and read aloud.

I just wanted to let you know that Dad and I contacted the police about what was stolen from Serena. Of course, we didn't mention exactly what was taken, only that thieves were preying on tourists on both Kauai and Maui, and that thefts had even happened on our cruises.

The thieves were caught and when the arrest was made, a seal pelt was discovered among the loot. The thieves claimed it was a magical artifact taken from a selkie, but no one believed them. The police saw it as evidence of the slaughter of Hawaiian Monk seals, an endangered species.

Dad says the judge will throw the book at them for that!

Now that Serena's family knows where her lost item is, they'll be able to get it back ... but not until after the trial. The family is anxious for those men to be imprisoned.

Hope everything in Colorado is great!

Your friend,
Maris

I folded the letter and smiled at Jed. "We're friends with a siren."

He nodded. "Not to mention a whole colony of selkies." He grinned and pulled me into his arms. "Who'd've ever guessed we'd be friends with any species of Fae?"

"Certainly not me," I said. "Life is full of surprises."

"Definitely," he said, hugging me even more tightly, "and I can't wait to discover the next one!"

COPYRIGHT

DANGEROUS DAZE

1

My name is Dani Erickson and I'm a demon hunter.

Of course, I'm also a sixteen-year-old girl and a junior at Longmont High School, but that's just my age and place in normal society. Demon hunter is a much better description, because it not only tells you who I am, but what I was born to do.

See, I'm not just some delusional teen who likes to imagine that I'm a hero, or a girl who likes to indulge in cosplay. I'm an honest to goodness, born and bred, hereditary demon hunter. I'm the seventh child of a seventh child, and up until my fourteenth birthday, I was clueless about the existence of demons or how the accident of my birth order gave me a unique destiny.

Fortunately (but not accidentally), my guardians appeared just as my abilities manifested. Warwick James (Wick to his friends, of which I am one) and Madame Simone became my teachers, confidantes, and friends. Wick taught me to fight and provided me with weapons, while Madam Simone gave me the arcane knowledge necessary to defeat an enemy that normal people can't even see. They became like second parents to me.

And what about my real parents? The folks who brought me into this world and gave me this destiny? The totally normal, middle-class American couple who raised me with love and appropriate boundaries?

They're totally clueless about my demon hunting ways, and I work very hard to keep them that way, thank you very much!

Same goes for my siblings, my six older brothers ... except for one. Jamie, my youngest older brother, discovered my secret when a demon lord kidnapped him and used him as bait to lure me into a trap. Unfortunately, the monster held Jamie prisoner near the portal he'd created to enter our world and bring his minions through. Proximity to a portal is necessary for a normal to see demons, so Jamie was exposed to the arcane world. He also saw me, his little sister, kick demon butt and destroy the creatures with sword and knives. Very skillfully, I might add.

Jamie was suitably impressed, and agreed to not only keep my secret, but to train with me so I didn't have to pretend to be taking ballet lessons with Allie in order to work with Wick.

Occasionally, older brothers can be useful. Sometimes even helpful. But now that the crisis has passed, Jamie can't see demons anymore than Allie can.

Who is Allie? Just the absolute BEST best friend a girl can have. Especially a girl who's also a demon hunter. Allie (Alejandra Chavez if you want to get all formal) is petite and pretty, graceful and popular. She's a true girly-girl, meaning she's everything I'm not ... and everything my parents have always wished I could be. But even though we're complete opposites, she's also my very best friend. The only person besides Jamie who knows who I truly am, and who, even though she's a norm and can't see demons, believes me and trusts me and helps me in any way she can.

Allie totally rocks!

2

_____

The front doorbell rang, and I glanced at the clock on the bedside table in my too-pink-and-prissy-to-be-believed bedroom. Allie was right on time, but I needed to get my butt in gear if we were going to avoid being late to school. I grabbed my favorite denim jacket (the one with a prowling lion embroidered on the back), the specially designed backpack Wick had given me, and raced down the stairs in my favorite knee-high boots — also specially designed for me by the artisans in Wick's clan of guardians.

"I've got it, Mom," I yelled as I skidded to a stop at the front door and yanked it open.

As expected, Allie stood on the porch playing with the end of her oh-so-chic French braid. Allie's hair looked great no matter how she wore it — long and straight and shining black, but that braid was eye-popping.

My own nut-brown hair had grown out and was now long enough to braid (which I did when I was training), but it never looked chic. More often than not, my not-quite-straight but not-really-curly locks frayed out of whatever I tried to do with them and just looked messy. But I'd never been really concerned with my looks, so I could admire Allie's easy beauty with only a trace of female jealousy.

I joined Allie on the porch and was just pulling the door closed when Mom appeared. "And just where do you think you're going, young lady?" she asked.

"Uhm … to school," I replied with a sideways glance at Allie. "You know, it's that time of the morning."

Mom scowled at the flip remark. "I didn't see you in the kitchen," she said. "What did you have for breakfast?"

"Seriously, Mom? I'm sixteen years old and you're still monitoring my eating habits?"

"You may be a high school junior," she said with a prim purse to her mouth, "but I'm still your mother."

"Fine," I said. "I didn't eat yet, but I don't have time now. We're going to be late."

"It's okay, Mrs. Erickson," Allie said, jumping in before things got out of control, "I have a bagel in my backpack for her. I've learned to come prepared."

Mom smiled at Allie. "You are too sweet, Allie," she said, her voice suddenly soft and sugary (blech!), "but you shouldn't be responsible for feeding my daughter." She turned her attention back to me and her eyes narrowed. "From now on, you're to get up a few minutes earlier so you have time to eat a proper breakfast … in *our* kitchen."

"Yes, ma'am," I mumbled and escaped off the porch.

Allie kept quiet until we were across the street and on the path through Loomiller Park, then she burst out laughing.

"What's so funny?" I practically growled.

"You!" She ended her giggle with a most unladylike snort. "You should've seen your face! Dani Heleen Erickson, Demon Hunter Extraordinaire, busted for not eating her breakfast … like a five-year-old!"

"Ha-ha," I snarled. "I'm *so* happy I could entertain you." I walked a few more steps, then held out my hand. "Hand it over."

"What?" she asked, her eyes going all wide and innocent.

"The bagel," I snapped.

She chortled, but swung her backpack around, opened a front pocket, and produced a cream cheese slathered bagel wrapped in a pretty pink cloth napkin. "Here you go, your highness."

I accepted my breakfast with as much dignity as I could muster, which wasn't much considering my mouth was actually watering. "Thanks," I said, and bit into the still warm treat. "You really are the best!"

By the time we'd crossed the park and made it onto school property, I'd finished eating. We waved to friends as they drove past on their way to the parking lot behind the school. You'd think Allie or I would be driving too—I mean, we're both sixteen, we have our licenses—but neither set of our parents thought we needed to drive to school when we lived so close. Besides, as both our mothers pointed out on a regular basis, walking is excellent exercise.

As we sauntered up the sidewalk to the main entrance, Brittney Dahl pushed past us, knocking Allie off balance. If I hadn't been right beside her, my BFF might have fallen. As it was, I caught her arm and steadied her while she got her feet back under her.

Once Allie was stable, I ran after Brittney, grabbed her elbow, and whirled her around. "Hey, Britt," I said, working to keep my anger under control. "You want to watch where you're going. You almost knocked Allie flat!"

Brittney glanced at Allie, then back at me. "So?" she said in her snottiest voice. "Isn't she supposed to be a dancer? She should have better balance."

My temper snapped. "Why you little..."

But Brittney didn't wait to hear my comment. She pulled

away from me and hurried through the front door and out of sight.

"Never mind," said Allie, coming to stand beside me. "No real harm done. Just be glad we don't have to put up with her on a regular basis."

I nodded, and we entered the building.

Longmont High was a pretty laid back, easy going place. Most of the kids got along, and the place had a nice, relaxed feel ... due in large part to my presence.

No. Really. I don't mean to brag, but LHS was a great place as high schools went because I kept the demon population to a minimum. When I first arrived, not too long after I'd come into my ability to see and fight demons, I'd discovered that most of my classmates (and many of my teachers) were demon-ridden. They had nasty little demons riding on their backs or shoulders sucking their life force and filling their minds with evil suggestions.

I put my training to work and dealt with enough of the vermin that most of them now avoided LHS. Hence the pleasant environment.

But not every human failure can be attributed to supernatural causes. Some people are just mean, and Brittney was one of them. She had never been a friend, not even to Allie, and Allie was one of those people who was universally loved. Well, almost. As I said, Britt didn't even get along with Allie.

I'd never understood what her problem was. She was a pretty blonde (when she wasn't scowling), her parents were wealthy (she always had the most fashionable clothes and the latest tech), and as far as anyone knew, her home life was great. So why did she feel the need to be such a complete and total grumpus?

Whatever. I had more than enough on my plate without

worrying about Brittney. As long as she stayed in her corner, I'd stay in mine.

"See you at lunch," Allie said with a little wave.

I grinned and the two of us moved off to our respective classes.

Later, my weird-o-meter registered the presence of a dangerous, high level demon in my vicinity. I was in phys ed at the time, jogging around the track in my dorky blue shorts and white T with the rest of my classmates. I slowed to a walk and scanned the area, turning slowly to give myself a three-sixty view. He stood in the parking lot, beyond a chain link fence, at the south end of the track. To normal eyes, he looked like a distinguished older gentleman — steel gray hair, clean shaven, wearing a dark colored business suit with a red power tie—but I saw past the glamour. I saw a six-foot tall demon with deep red scales, back-curving horns, and a prehensile tail that ended in a blade-like triangular tip.

He met my gaze and smiled. At least, the glamour smiled; his actual expression was closer to a leer.

My heart raced and my breath became shallow. Adrenaline pumped through my system and it was all I could do not to sprint for the fence and tear my way through. I wanted to fight. I wanted to destroy this unnatural fiend who had dared venture onto my school grounds!

But that wouldn't be smart. I was dressed for phys ed, not for battle. I didn't have my weapons, and while after two and a half years of training I could take out the little personal demons without a weapon, a demon lord like this guy would require serious effort, and probably some planning.

No, the battle would have to wait. He was on my radar now. We'd meet again, and if possible, I'd have Wick by my side when that happened.

As if reading my decision, he gave me a little salute, and

3

_I_ grabbed Allie after school and practically dragged her across the park to my home. Demon imps danced just out of my reach for the entire trek, and even though I was armed and dangerous now, I ignored them. I had to get home, get the car, and get to Wick.

"What's the rush, Dani?" Allie panted as she trotted beside me. I'm a lot taller, so my stride is longer. Plus, when I'm in a hurry, I can _move_.

"I'll explain when we get to the dojo," I said, gritting my teeth and clamping down of the desire to play _whack-a-demon_.

When we reached the safety of my family's property (demons can't set foot on a demon hunter's land), I raced into the house, while Allie followed at a more sedate pace.

"Hey, Mom," I called, unloading school books from my backpack onto a long library table in the hallway.

"Hi, sweetheart," she answered, appearing at the other end of the hall. "You're home earlier than I expected."

"Hi, Mrs. Erickson," Allie said, following me down the hall.

"I'm sorry, Allie," Mom said with a smile. "I didn't see you."

"That happens a lot when I'm standing behind Dani," my best friend quipped.

I threw a scowl at her, but didn't respond. We stepped into our warm, sunny kitchen and I made a beeline for the row of hooks where the car keys were kept.

"What are you girls up to this afternoon?" Mom asked, narrowing her eyes as she watched me grab the keys to our older Subaru Outback. The old blue vehicle was manufactured before the turn of the century (the twenty-first century), but it was reliable, got great gas mileage, and the insurance was cheap, even for teenage drivers. Mom and Dad kept it as our "starter" car, and each of us kids had been given driving privileges to it as we earned our licenses.

Since Jamie was now in his freshman year at the University of Colorado, Boulder and lived on campus, the Subaru was my car exclusively.

"Allie and I are headed to the dojo," I said, keeping my voice casual even though I could see demon imps dancing in the neighbors yard where it abutted our property. "I have a couple of new moves I want to show off."

Mom's expression lightened. She and Dad had given me permission to take classes with Wick, all because Jamie had made a big deal of wanting to learn martial arts and had convinced them that I should join him. After all, a girl needed to learn self-defense in this day and age.

Even though Jamie was living in Boulder now, I continued to train ... with their blessing. Exercise was to be encouraged, and the parental units had been impressed both with the discipline of Wick's students and with Wick himself.

"That's very sweet of you, Allie," Mom said, "taking an interest in Dani's martial arts training."

"No biggie," Allie answered. "After all, Dani comes to my

ballet recitals." She gave me an evil grin. "Plus, some of the guys she trains with are *hot!*"

I glared at her, but Mom just laughed and shook her head. "Only you would make a remark like that to me, Allie." She glanced at me and patted my cheek. "Don't be mortified, Dani. I know there are cute boys at the dojo. After all, Jamie used to be one of them!"

Allie blushed and I made a quick twirling motion with my finger so she'd turn around before Mom noticed.

"Thanks, Mom," I said and kissed her cheek. "We've gotta run." And I hustled Allie down the hall and out the front door.

"Drive carefully," Mom called after us.

Allie and I tossed our backpacks in the back seat and climbed into the car. Once we were safely inside, I said, "You should've seen your face! The mere mention of Jamie and you light up like a Christmas tree."

Jamie and Allie had been thrown together a lot in the past couple of years. Being my co-conspirators in the world of demon-hunting gave them a lot to think about, and no one they could discuss it with except me ... and each other.

After Jamie and Allie spent a terrifying half-hour barricaded in Wick's office while Wick and I battled a demon lord and his herd of minions last year, they'd realized they had more in common than just me. There was a strong physical attraction between them. They'd been dating steadily ever since.

And I couldn't be happier. My youngest older brother and my best friend in the whole world. What could be better? As long as Jamie didn't do anything stupid like hurt Allie, all was well.

If he ever did hurt her, well, let's just say that my Ninja skills could be used for more than fighting demons.

Allie sighed. "It's stupid, I know, but I miss him so much."

"He's just in Boulder," I reminded her. "Fifteen miles is nothing."

She rolled her eyes. "For you, maybe. You have a car. I don't, and neither does Jamie. At least, not this year."

I turned from Francis Street onto 9th Avenue and headed east toward Main Street. "Ugh. Don't remind me! If he gets a parking permit for CU next year, I may lose my car." I patted the dashboard affectionately. "And you like me better, don't you, Subie?"

Allie giggled. "You're a nut. You know that, don't you?"

"Pulled you out of your romantic funk, didn't I? Besides," I said with a quick sideways glance at my friend, "it's April. School will be out in early June. Jamie will be home before you know it."

I parked in front of Wick's dojo and glanced up and down the street. "No demons in sight. We're clear to go."

We jumped out of the car, locked the doors, and were across the sidewalk in mere moments. The bell over the door jingled as we stepped through the wards and into the safety of my guardian's martial arts academy. Wick emerged from his office at the rear of the large practice floor looking calm and unsurprised to see us.

Tall and trim, with great muscle tone, Wick was good looking, for a guy almost old enough to be my father. He sported short brown hair, a neatly trimmed mustache and beard, and his blue-green eyes were clear and honest. He'd trained me, fought beside me and been wounded in defense of those I loved.

I trusted Wick with my life. Literally.

"Miss Erickson. Miss Chavez. I'm pleased to see you, of course," he said as he crossed the room to meet us, "but as I wasn't expecting you, I must ask, what brings you here today?"

"I've been wondering the same thing," Allie said. "Dani's being very mysterious about this visit."

I ignored the jibe, and focused on my guardian. "We have a

4

*A*llie gasped.

Wick frowned and glanced from me to Allie and back again. "And how is this Brittney Dahl significant?"

Allie answered before I could compose my thoughts.

"She's not a nice girl. A bully, really, and she dislikes both Dani and me."

I nodded. "To be honest, she dislikes everyone ... and pretty much everyone dislikes her right back."

"But she seems to *really* dislike us," Allie finished.

"I see," Wick said. He met my gaze. "And she's not demon ridden?"

I shook my head. "She had one, but I got rid of it. I expected that to make a difference, but it didn't. Not really."

Wick tapped his chin. "Interesting. Of course, demons aren't the only reason for human misbehavior. Some people are sociopaths, or even psychopaths, by nature, but there are fewer of them than popularly believed."

He paced back and forth across the practice floor, thinking, while Allie and I stuffed our backpacks into the cubbies that lined the wall for his students' use. Then we took our places on a mat, sitting tailor fashion while we waited for him to speak.

After another couple of passes, Wick dropped to the mat facing us.

"When did this take place? You said he was in the parking lot. Was it before school or after school?"

"Neither," I replied. "It was during my phys ed class, after lunch. We were running laps on the track. He was just on the other side of the fence from me."

"And did he take notice of you?"

I nodded. "He looked straight at me, and smiled."

Wick scowled. "I don't like this. He chose your most vulnerable time to reveal himself: you were unarmed and away from the safety of your home." He paused and shook his head. "He's too well informed for my comfort."

He stood and began pacing again. After a moment he stopped and pointed at me. "You need to be on high alert, Miss Erickson. Go nowhere unarmed. Find a way to stay out of phys ed until this is resolved. I will shadow you as closely as possible. If you feel his presence, go home. Don't ask for permission, just leave. We'll find a way to clear things up with the school later, but your priority must be personal safety."

Wick was scaring me, which given the seriousness of his expression was probably exactly what he intended. But I didn't like being scared. I also didn't like running away from a fight. I wasn't a green demon hunter anymore. I'd been fighting monsters for more than two years, and I'd even gone up against a couple of demon lords.

Of course, Wick had been badly wounded in our last encounter with one of the big-wigs of the demon world. Was it possible my guardian was afraid?

I studied Wick as he took a seat on the mat again. Yes, he looked grim, his face set in a deadly serious expression, but his eyes were calm and his voice hadn't shaken. His hands were steady as he folded them in his lap, and he met my gaze levelly.

No. Wick was cautious, but not frightened. The precautions he was suggesting weren't coming from a place of fear. He was, as he had said, safeguarding my continued existence.

But I had to ask, "Why are we avoiding the fight? Why don't we just drop Allie at home, hunt this demon down, and destroy him?"

"Because we don't know what he's up to," Wick answered promptly. He knew me well enough to expect the question. " He allowed you to see him on the school grounds, and he made sure you knew of his connection to Miss Dahl. He has a larger plan in mind, and we'll be better served to deal with the consequences if we know what it is." He skewered me with his gaze. "So for now, we wait and watch and maintain security."

He held my gaze until I nodded, and then turned to Allie.

"You must also be on guard, Miss Chavez." Allie's eyes widened and a pretty pink blush stained her cheeks. "You've been targeted before and would make an excellent hostage to use against Miss Erickson."

Allied nodded. "I'll be careful, and I'll stay away from strange men."

"Excellent," Wick said, clapping his hands together. "If you'll wait here while I pull my Jeep around front, we'll all leave together and I'll follow you home to make sure you arrive safely."

5

*T*he next morning I dressed quickly, inspected my blades before sheathing them, and packed a supply of holy water in my backpack, then I ran down the stairs to the kitchen.

"Here I am," I said as I crossed the room and kissed Mom on the cheek. "Ready and willing to eat breakfast at the kitchen table."

Mom beamed. "See? That wasn't so hard, was it?"

"Nope," I said, reaching into one of the hickory cabinets and extracting my favorite cereal, a calorie laden combination of sugar coated wheat flakes and big fat raisins.

The kitchen was the heart of our home. Its terra cotta red walls, pale lemon curtains, and light hickory cabinets gave it a warm and welcoming feel. Just like Mom, who had designed the kitchen and was its main inhabitant, was the heart of our family. The one who held us all together with her warmth and love.

She might be a stern disciplinarian, and she definitely expected all of us to toe the line and obey the house rules, but all of us kids knew that she'd give her very life to protect any one of us. Yeah, I could make time to eat breakfast in the kitchen if it made Mom happy.

After I'd slurped down my cereal and milk, had my daily vitamin C in the form of a glass of orange juice, and loaded my dirty dishes into the dishwasher, I grabbed my backpack.

"I'm off to school, Mom," I said, heading toward the front door. If I hurried, I might make it onto the porch before Allie rang the doorbell.

"Have a good day," Mom called.

Allie was just turning the corner when I pulled the front door closed behind me. I waved and raced down the steps to join her on the sidewalk. Scanning the park across the street, I noted the complete absence of demons. I frowned. That wasn't normal. Usually there were a couple hanging out the trees, just watching our house. As long as they didn't bother anyone, I left them alone.

But this morning, even the sentries were gone.

"What's wrong, Dani?" Allie asked as we followed the path across the park.

"Nothing."

"Uh-huh," she said, giving me her *I-don't-think-so* expression. "Then why are you frowning."

"It's just that there isn't a single demon in the park," I explained. "There are usually at least a couple of the little guys around."

"And that's a bad thing?" she asked in a puzzled voice.

"No. Not a bad thing," I admitted. "Just out of the ordinary." I didn't add what I was thinking, that I didn't like out of the ordinary when there was a demon lord on the loose.

When we got to the school entrance, our path was blocked. Students milled around outside the doors, but no one was going in.

"What's happening?" Allie asked a guy near us.

He shrugged. "No idea. I just know the doors are still locked. No one can get into the building."

Allie and I shared a startled glance. Yet another out-of-the-ordinary occurrence.

Just then the students took a collective step back, and Allie and I hurried to conform. One of the doors opened and Principal Jerrold appeared holding a cordless microphone.

"Attention, students," he said, and the crowd quieted immediately. "We've had an incident on school grounds. The police are here and we'll be starting our day a little late due to security measures that the Longmont Police Department has put in place for your protection."

A buzz of conversation began and Allie took the opportunity to lean toward me and whisper, "Do you think this has anything to do with, you know, *him*?"

Principal Jerrold continued before I could answer. "Everyone will need to enter through this one door," he explained. "You'll be checked through into the school by a uniformed officer. Once you're inside, please proceed directly to your homeroom. Do not linger in the hallways."

He turned and glanced through the glass doors, nodded, and turned back to us. "We're ready to begin. Please form a single line and remain calm. Your teachers will brief you on the situation as soon as everyone is inside and in their assigned classrooms. Thank you for your cooperation."

More students had arrived while Principal Jerrold spoke, so Allie and I were now in the middle of the crowd. Everyone jostled around until we were in a line that stretched along the sidewalk and into the parking lot. A few teachers patrolled the line. They didn't answer questions, but their presence ensured our good behavior while we waited.

Finally, Allie and I reached the head of the line. A police officer stood just outside the door, watching the line. Two more were inside between the door and a table staffed by school personnel with laptop computers. A light flare on the glass kept me from seeing much beyond that point.

Allie entered first and I followed right behind her ... and immediately wished I was back outside.

I was in a chokepoint with no escape. No way to go except forward, and what waited in front of me would be my downfall.

Beyond the table with the computers and the staff with strained expressions on their faces stood a metal detector like the ones at the Denver airport. Manned by additional police officers.

And I was wearing stiletto blades in my boots and had a short sword concealed in my backpack.

I was toast.

I grabbed Allie's shoulder as the guy ahead of her approached the table and handed over his school ID. "Once you're clear," I whispered, "call Wick. I'm going to need him."

She gave me a startled look, but nodded. After the last demon lord had tried to lure Allie into danger in a coffee shop, we'd all agreed that she should have Wick's number. I'd programmed it into her cell phone myself.

Allie had half turned to ask me a question, when one of the staff called, "Next!" She approached the table and handed over her ID.

I sweated out the wait. I couldn't do anything else. No way out.

Once my ID had been checked, I licked my lips and walked to my doom. The young officer who held out his hand for my backpack didn't look much older than me. After a tiny hesitation, I handed it over. Another officer beckoned me forward and pointed through the metal detector.

"Step through, please."

I glanced at Allie, who waited on the other side. If only I could magically transport across the space to join her!

The young officer with my backpack yelled, "Sir!" just as I stepped into the detector. Alarms screamed. The officer at the door slammed it shut as all four of the other uniformed men rushed to surround me, guns drawn.

I met Allie's gaze, and she answered my silent plea with a nod. Wick would come. He had to!

6

My stilettos and short sword were confiscated. I was patted down for additional weapons, hand-cuffed, marched from the building, and stuffed into the back seat of a police cruiser. All in plain view of my classmates.

When we arrived at the police station, the cuffs were removed and I was locked in a gray-walled room with a huge mirror on one wall. I'd seen enough police shows on television to assume it was one-way glass. I sat alone in the sparsely furnished room (just a metal table and three metal chairs) and tried not to tremble.

Carrying deadly weapons was no laughing matter, not in this age of school shootings and mass murders. I'd missed the explanation of the incident that had caused the police response, but I was enlightened during the course of my arrest. The anniversary of the Columbine High School shootings was approaching and the police department had received evidence of what they believed was a credible threat against Longmont High. They took it seriously, and I was the one caught in the trap. Me. The one person who was actively working to protect the school.

I suppose it could've been worse; I could've been carrying a rifle.

Not that the type of weapon would make a difference. Heck, a grade-schooler had been expelled for taking a kitchen knife to school to cut his birthday cake. And my blades were far more deadly than a kitchen knife.

What were my parents going to think? They didn't have a clue about those weapons ... or what I used them for. The only person other than Wick who'd ever seen me in action was Jamie, and he was in Boulder at CU.

Wick would help, of course, but I wasn't sure what he could do to protect me from law enforcement. I'd joked with him about getting expelled when he'd first given me the specially modified boots and backpack, but after two years of wearing them, I'd stopped worrying about that possibility. As Wick had said, "Better expelled than dead."

But now the worst had happened. I was about to be expelled, possibly imprisoned, and — even worse! — my secret identity was about to be exposed to my parents.

I repeat: I was toast.

The door opened and my parents were ushered in. Mom rushed to me and I stood for her hug. Dad glowered at the officer until the door swung closed, then he turned to me. I've seen Dad in a lot of moods, but I'd never seen such a jumbled mix of bewilderment, sadness, anger, and despair.

I wanted to disappear into the woodwork.

Mom still hugged me tightly. I hadn't realized she was crying until her tears soaked through my T-shirt. Gently, I extricated myself, feeling calmer than I had any right to. Now that the moment had come, my trembling ceased as my inner demon hunter took over. This was a different kind of danger, but I was always calm when the danger was deadliest.

"I don't understand, Dani," Dad said, stepping forward to give me a quick squeeze. "What were you doing with a sword?"

I nodded to the mirror and said quietly, "Not here."

Dad glanced at the mirror, clenched his jaw, and nodded. "Let's sit down. Our attorney should be here soon."

Since I was a minor with no prior record, I was released into my parents custody and a hearing date was set. As Mom and Dad herded me out of the building, I caught sight of Wick and Allie, and knew that they'd follow us home.

Good thing. I was going to need Wick's support when I tried to explain who and what I was to my parents.

We'd barely made it into the kitchen from the garage, when the doorbell rang. I started to answer when Mom laid a hand on my arm. "Let your father get it."

I stopped, nodded, and followed Mom to the scrubbed oak kitchen table. We sat as I strained to hear what was being said at the door. It was hopeless, all I could make out was a murmur of voices.

Footsteps echoed on the hardwood floor of the hall and Dad appeared followed by Wick and Allie. I jumped up and ran to my friends. Allie hugged me, while Wick stroked my back. I shivered with terror. Now that I was home and safe, my fear threatened to consume me.

Leaving me in Allie's arms, Wick stepped to my mother. "Mrs. Erickson, I don't know if you remember, but we met at Union Reservoir ... on Dani's fourteenth birthday."

I looked up from Allie's shoulder in time to see comprehension dawn on Mom's face. "Yes, I do remember. Dani had an odd episode, a little seizure, and you were able to calm her."

He nodded and turned to Dad. "I'm not just Dani's martial arts instructor."

Dad's eyes narrowed. "Why didn't we know about this connection before? Have you been stalking our daughter? Are you the reason she's in trouble now?"

Wick gestured to the table. "Why don't we all take a seat," he said, his voice calm and soothing, yet firm. "We have much to discuss, and some of it has been put off too long."

Mom looked confused, but took her place at the table. Dad looked like he wanted to yell at Wick for ordering him around in his own home, but he glanced at Mom and then at me, and sat.

Allie and I took our places next to each other and Wick pulled out a chair across from Mom and Dad.

"All right," Wick said, "Now that we're all settled, let's begin. Miss Erickson, do you wish to explain or should I?"

Dad opened his mouth, but Mom touched his hand and he closed it again.

"I think you'll do a better job, Wick," I said quietly.

He nodded. "Mr. Erickson, I know you're familiar with your father's beliefs regarding the seventh son of a seventh son."

Dad sighed, his brow furrowed. "Of course. It's utter nonsense, but that's got nothing to do with this."

"On the contrary," Wick said. "It has everything to do with this. Your father was only mistaken in believing that gender was an issue." Dad looked like he was about to interrupt, but Wick held up his hand and Dad subsided. "The seventh child of a seventh child is a powerfully potent individual, a hereditary demon hunter, born with the ability to see what others cannot, and, when properly trained, to dispatch the unholy creatures who prey on unknowing humans."

He paused a beat and then announced, "Your daughter is such a person."

Dad jumped up and lunged across the table at Wick. "You're insane," he bellowed. "You've been filling Dani's head with nonsense and now you've caused her to be in trouble with the law!"

I jumped up too. "Dad! Sit down. Wick's not to blame. You and Grandpa are!"

Dad froze, then slowly turned his head to stare at me. "What did you say to me?"

My demon hunting calm had returned. My pulse no longer raced, but was slow and steady, my nerves were steel. I knew what needed to be done.

"I said, 'you and Grandpa are to blame.' Now stop yelling at Wick and listen to us. Wick's done nothing but help and protect me. You're just now hearing about this because I've forbidden him to speak to you."

I gave Wick an apologetic bow, and turned to Allie. "Allie's known about my abilities almost from the start. She's helped me hide them from you. We used ballet and singing lessons to cover my training with Wick and Madam Simone."

I glared at both my parents, daring them to interrupt. My expression must have been fierce, because they just stared at me in silence.

"But none of this would've been necessary if Grandpa hadn't decided he needed to produce a seventh-seventh. Sure he got the gender wrong, but his breeding program worked." I stabbed my finger at Dad. "You're the seventh child. You're the one who could pass on the inheritance, not Uncle Gus. And the two of you," I widened my glare to include Mom, "decided to have seven children. You're the reason I'm who and what I am. Not Wick. It's not Wick's fault that I'm a seventh-seventh. That's all on you and Grandpa."

I took a deep breath and sat down. "Not that I'm complaining about being born," I muttered. "I'm just stating facts."

Dad clutched Mom's hand and inhaled a trembling breath. "S-so y-you're saying you believe this crap?"

"Believe it?" I asked, my voice declaring my incredulity. "Of course I believe it! I'm living it!"

I closed my eyes and counted to ten. I had to remember, they couldn't see demons, they had no way to prove or disprove what

Wick and I were telling them. I had to be patient. But at the same time, Allie was in the same boat, and she'd never doubted me.

Parents! They thought they knew everything.

I glanced at Wick, but he just raised an eyebrow and nodded for me to continue.

"Look," I said, schooling my voice to calm. "Do you remember when Jamie went missing? How I found him?"

Mom and Dad both nodded.

"Well, he wasn't exactly missing. I knew where he was instantly. I can tell where any member of my family is if I concentrate on them. I can also sense demons, where they are and what their relative strength is. It's one of the gifts Wick and Simone have been helping me master."

"Who is this Simone you keep talking about?" Mom asked.

Wick took that one for me. "Simone and I are part of an ancient clan of guardians. Our people monitor large families and watch for the advent of a hunter. We were both in Longmont for Dani's fourteenth birthday, which is when the power typically manifests, if it's going to."

"What do you mean, if it's going to?" I interrupted.

"There have been seventh-sevenths who have never manifested power. We don't understand why, but it happens occasionally. When it does, we leave the individual in ignorance."

"Lucky them," I muttered.

Wick stared at me until I met his gaze. "Would you really relinquish your gift, Miss Erickson?"

I continued to lock eyes with him while I considered the question. Would I give it up if I could? Would I return to being an unknowing victim of a race of unseen creatures? Would I be content to allow them to suck the life and joy from my family and friends?

"No," I said. Then with more strength, "I've come to terms

with my destiny. I'm a powerful demon hunter and it's my job to protect those in my domain. I wouldn't go back even if I could."

Wick nodded. "Very good, Miss Erickson. Please, continue with your tale."

"Wait a minute," Mom said. "So it wasn't an accident that you were at the reservoir on her birthday?"

"No, Mrs. Erickson. It was no accident."

"And the incident, Dani's seizure..."

"Was not a medical condition," Wick answered. "It was the advent of her power. She began training with me the next day."

"And why would she trust you and not us?" Dad asked, anger evident in his voice.

I started to speak, but Wick silenced me with a glance.

"Even if she had told you, Mr. Erickson, you would've been unable to help her. You are not a seventh-seventh, nor are you genetically related to the guardian clan. She needed *us*. We can see demons. We can fight demons. But we can't destroy them, nor can we repair the rents in time and space that allow them to enter our world. Only a demon hunter possesses those abilities, and they are all too rare in this age of small families. Dani is a treasure that our world desperately needs."

"As to why she didn't tell you," Allie said, speaking for the first time, and with surprising ferocity, "I'd like to answer that." She stood and faced my parents. All five-two of her. "I really like you, Mr. and Mrs. Erickson, but I've watched you try to mold Dani into a girly-girl for as long as I've known her. 'Don't be a tom-boy, Dani. We have enough boys in this family, Dani.'" She mimicked my family's mantras rather cruelly, but very accurately. "I've thought for a long time that someone should smack you and make you realize that she's perfect just the way she is. She doesn't need to be a mini me. She's Dani, and she's awesome."

Allie sat quickly, looking suddenly embarrassed by her

outburst.

Mom's cheeks flamed and Dad looked like an innocuous pet hamster had bitten him and drawn blood. They both glanced at me and then lowered their eyes.

"Look," I said quietly. "I love you both, and you're the best parents in the world, but you do try to put me in a box where I don't fit ... and when my power manifested, I finally understood that I'll never fit and why. I can't be a sweet little princess. I have to be an Amazon warrior. I'm a fighter; it's my heritage, my destiny." I took a deep breath and blurted, "And while we're being honest, can we please redecorate my bedroom? I hate pink!"

Mom looked ready to cry, but Dad burst out laughing. "That's the first thing you've said that I understand!" When he had himself under control, he wiped his eyes and asked, "What were you saying about Jamie?"

"Oh. Right." I took a deep breath and ripped off the Band-Aid. "Jamie was kidnapped by demons to bait a trap to take me out." Mom looked ready to deny what I was saying, so I raced on. "They held him close enough to their portal that he could see them. He knows they exist."

"What?" my parents yelped in unison.

"But he's okay because Wick and I went after him. Wick got Jamie out—or tried to, Wick was injured in the attempt—while I took out the demon horde. Call Jamie, have him come home. He'll tell you what he saw."

"I've never seen a demon," Allie said into the silence, "but Wick and Dani barricaded me and Jamie into Wick's office once last year to protect us while they battled a bunch of them." Allie shivered, and then continued quietly, "The things we heard ... it was terrifying, and when Dani yelled that we could come out, Wick was unconscious and his chest was burned so badly we were really worried. I helped with some first aid until Madame

Simone arrived. She has a special gift for healing supernatural wounds."

"Oh my God!" Mom exclaimed. "Dani! How could you have put yourself in such danger and not let us know?"

I sighed. "How could I tell you when I knew you wouldn't believe me?"

Dad called Jamie, and my brother dropped everything, caught a ride with a friend, and came home to support me. He arrived before dinner.

Jamie told Mom and Dad everything he knew. He wasn't a kid anymore, he was a college man, and while he apologized to my parents for not telling them, he stated simply that it wasn't his truth to tell and that he respected me too much to betray my confidence.

Color me amazed.

We had a good old fashioned family hug, and agreed to let bygones be bygones. What was needed now was a good strategy for moving forward.

Wick and Allie came back after dinner. Jamie met Allie with a hug, and then settled down next to her at the kitchen table, our designated war room.

Dad shook hands with Wick, thanked him for his service to the Erickson kids, and told Wick to consider himself part of our family. Dad also asked if he could sit in on one of my training sessions. He wanted to see how his daughter handled herself.

Wick had an idea about how to deal with the weapons

charges against me. Obviously, we couldn't tell the police the truth. They'd never believe my blades were used to defend my classmates and teachers from demons. Lets face it, Mom and Dad were having enough trouble with that information ... and they loved me.

"You may not realize that I've been teaching a self-defense class at the high school," Wick told my parents. "It was a way for me to be on campus and available in the early days when your daughter was first learning to handle things. At this point, there's not much need. Miss Erickson has pretty well cleared the school of personal demons. They now recognize it as being under her protection and steer clear."

"Seriously?" Dad asked.

"Definitely," Jamie answered. "Longmont High has a much nicer atmosphere since Dani arrived. Once I was introduced to the demon population, I understood why that was, but all my friends noticed the change. They just didn't attribute it to Dani's presence."

"Okay," said Dad, looking stunned, "but how does that help us now."

"Well," Wick continued, "I thought I might be able to go to the authorities and tell them that Miss Erickson is a gifted martial artist, and that I asked her to bring her blades to school so that we could give a demonstration to my self-defense classes, a kind of advertisement of the kind of advanced training they might aspire to learn."

He paused and looked around expectantly. "Well, what do you think?"

Mom and Dad exchanged glances. Finally, Dad said, "I don't know if that would excuse her carrying concealed weapons, especially since everyone has seen her with those boots and that backpack practically on a daily basis, but it's sure worth a try."

"Definitely," said Jamie. "Lots of people know she trains with you, and I can testify that she works with weapons. I do too."

"And," added Allie, "no one can prove that the blades have been in her boots and backpack any other time. I mean, I'm with her every day and I've never seen them at school."

"Excellent," said Wick. "I'll go to the police station first thing in the morning and make a statement."

A warm glow of contentment filled my soul. Mom and Dad knew my secret, and they still loved me. If anything, they felt bad that I hadn't felt safe enough to confide in them. Jamie loved me enough to cut classes and come home to defend me. Allie had told off my parents in my defense, and Wick had come up with a possible strategy to explain my apparent misconduct.

Maybe I wouldn't be expelled from high school and sent to prison after all. Maybe everything would work out.

The doorbell rang, and we all looked at each other. No one was expecting visitors.

Dad got up and strode down the hall. Jamie followed at a distance.

A moment later Jamie was back. "It's the police," he said. "They're here for Dani."

Everyone stood.

Dad returned to the kitchen, his expression grim, followed by two uniformed officers and two plain clothes types.

One of the plain clothes guys stepped forward and flipped open a badge case. "I'm Detective Schaffer and this is my partner, Detective Hobson. Homicide."

While he spoke, his partner circled the table to stand beside me. "Dani Heleen Erickson, you're under arrest for the murder of Brittney Dahl."

"What?" I yelled as he pulled my hands behind my back and cuffed them for the second time that day. "What do you mean? What happened to Britt?"

"Wait just a minute," Dad called. "You can't arrest her again. The judge released her into our custody!"

"That was for a weapons charge," Detective Schaffer said. "This is for murder. She's coming with us."

The uniformed officers ran interference while the detectives perp marched me out of my home and stuffed me into a police cruiser ... again.

So much for everything working out.

8

*Y*ou haven't lived until you've spent a night in jail.

Believe me, I don't want to live that way again. Ever.

By this time, I'd seen a lot of demons, but I'd never seen that many fat, sassy, self-assured demons attached to as many ugly, mean-spirited people. And me without my weapons.

Fortunately, because of my youth, I was placed in solitary, but I could still hear the cat calls and the demonic taunts. What a miserable experience, and unless I was very, very lucky, I might be getting a foretaste of my entire future.

Brittney Dahl was dead. I'd never liked the girl, but I hadn't wished her dead, just far away from me and mine.

Wick came to visit me the next morning and gave me the details he and Simone had ferreted out. Britt's throat had been cut with a sharp-edged instrument, just like one of my blades. Her body had been found stuffed in a shack behind the football stadium when the police were clearing the grounds at the high school. The coroner determined that she'd died sometime around midnight on the night before I was arrested the first time.

And the most damaging of all? The police found an entry in her diary stating that I'd called and asked her to meet me at that time and place.

"Why would she write that?" I asked Wick. "I've never called her, and I've certainly never asked her to meet me anywhere."

"Of course not," Wick said in that calm voice of his. "But you did see her with a demon lord. One who undoubtedly sent the police that credible threat that caused your blades to be discovered, and one who probably dictated exactly what she was to write. Poor girl had no idea she was sealing her own death with that entry."

My heart fluttered and my stomach roiled with nausea. Yeah, I was sorry Britt was dead, but I was a lot sorrier that she'd framed me. Of course, she hadn't known she was framing me for murder, but still, she'd disliked me enough to go along with whatever scheme the demon lord had sold to her.

"I'm going to prison aren't I?" I asked, feeling my options drying up.

"No," Wick said with such assurance that my mouth dropped open.

"Close your mouth, Miss Erickson," he said with a grim little smile. "You're far too valuable to waste away in prison. Yes, you could probably make life easier for the inmates and reduce their recidivism to almost nothing, but the non-criminal world needs your services too badly to limit the scope of your work to a single prison."

"Okay," I said. "I like the sound of that. I just don't know how you're going to get me released."

"My clan is working on it," he said, matter of factly. "Your parents have been apprised that a guardian will appear as your defense attorney and that they are to accept whoever steps forward, as long as I vouch for that person. You will do the same. Agreed?"

"Agreed."

"And if all else fails, know that you will be rescued from this place. No matter what the criminal justice system decides, you will not be incarcerated more than a few days. Understood?

I swallowed, thought about asking what he meant, but decided I didn't want to know. "Understood."

"Chin up, Miss Erickson. All will be well."

9

The next few weeks were the worst of my life.

Because of the seriousness of the crime, I wasn't allowed bail. I remained in jail, quarantined from the rest of the world.

The lawyer the clan provided was a wonderful woman, warm and caring when she spoke with me, fierce in my defense, and from the expressions I saw on the prosecutors' faces, she knew the law better than they had anticipated. She was well versed in obscure cases, ones that even the judge had to research.

And my family ... what can I say? The Ericksons, from Mom and Dad and all my brothers all the way up to Grandpa, know how to stand up for their own. Everyone was verbal in my defense, each of my brothers was willing to be interviewed at a moment's notice about how their little sister was not only innocent, she was incapable of murder.

I had to smile every time I saw Jamie do such an interview. He was always careful to qualify his statement, that I was absolutely incapable of taking a *human* life. If anyone else noticed his qualification, I never heard about it.

But despite their unwavering support and my lawyer's brilliance, when the moment came, I was convicted.

The courtroom exploded in a wave of angry outbursts from my family and friends ... and then, absolute silence reigned.

Everyone froze in exactly the position they'd been in when the spell was activated.

I recognized the time spell. I'd used it often enough at Longmont High to battle demons while my classmates and teachers hung in suspended animation. I turned around looking for the caster, and found several people still animated, as well as a multitude of demons, from tiny personal ones that rode their human victims to bouncing imps, excited by seeing a hunter in trouble. But they were all low-level creatures and kept a wary distance from those of us who could not only see them, but could end their miserable existences.

Of the humans in the room, only four besides myself were mobile.

My lawyer.

Wick.

Simone.

And a young man I'd never seen before.

Of course. Members of the guardian clan would be as immune to the spell as I was. Simone had been the one who taught me to stop time.

The four of them gathered around me.

"What's going on?" I asked.

Wick smiled. "I told you we would not allow you to waste your life in prison, Miss Erickson," he said. "Allow me to introduce Gregorio Radovan. As I'm sure you've deduced, Greg is a member of the guardian clan. He will guide you to a safe haven."

"Hi," I said, feeling more than a little off-balance. Greg was only a couple of years older than me and seriously cute, with curly light brown hair and blue eyes that twinkled with mischief.

He held out his hand. "A pleasure, Miss Erickson. I look forward to working with you."

I accepted his hand, and he raised my knuckles to his lips and pressed a kiss to them. My heart raced and my cheeks blazed. He released my hand and stepped back beside Wick.

I wanted to fan myself, but managed to quash the impulse.

My attorney was speaking, and I forced my attention to her.

"We wanted to clear your name," she said, "so that you could remain here with your family, but that's no longer possible. Your life in this community, in this state, is over, Miss Erickson."

"I – What?" I said.

"You will have no further contact with any member of your family, Dani," Simone said gently. "If you ever return to this place, it will be many, many years from now. You are a citizen of the world now, Dani."

"But, I can't..." I closed my eyes and took a deep breath. When I opened them again, I'd called up my demon hunter calm. "I need to say good-bye. I can't just disappear."

"I'm afraid you must, Miss Erickson," Wick said. "Think about what you've been taught. If we release the time stop, we release it for everyone, and this will have been for nothing."

"We've brought Greg in to guide you because he is unknown," my lawyer said. "Wick and Simone and I will remain in place. We will be as astonished as everyone else by your disappearance. In a few days, I will go back to my practice in Washington, D.C."

"Simone and I will remain in Longmont for a time," Wick said. "In a year or two, I will close my dojo and move on."

"But I will remain here with your family," Simone said, picking up the tale. "To the outside world, it will appear that your mother has turned to new age spirituality after the unexplained disappearance of her youngest child. She will consult with me on a regular basis. Your father will seem to disapprove, but will not have the heart to deny her this source of comfort."

"In reality," she continued, "I will act as a conduit for you to communicate with your loved ones. You must never write or phone them, but the clan will relay messages to me and I will pass them along to your family. They will know that you are alive and well and fulfilling your destiny."

My eyes filled with tears, and I searched the faces of each member of my family. Not their best looks, frozen as they had been in the midst of crying, shouting, or shaking fists. But all those expressions spoke of their love for me. Their belief in my innocence. Their determination to have me free and happy and healthy and at home with them.

I memorized each of them, these people who had filled my life with love and joy and, occasionally aggravation — after all, SIX brothers! — and who I would miss every day for the rest of my life.

The clan offered me freedom and health, and probably even happiness, but I would never again know my first and best home. I was grieving already.

"I'm so sorry, Miss Erickson," Wick said. He folded me in his arms and held me close. "A hug from your father," he whispered, and I burst into tears.

EPILOGUE

A new chapter in my life has begun. I'm still Dani Erickson, still me, but I'm no longer a high school student or a citizen of Colorado. I'm not even sure I'm still a citizen of the United States. Simone spoke truly: I'm a citizen of the world now.

Greg and I are currently somewhere in the Carpathian Mountains of Romania traveling with a band of the guardian clan. I'm learning a new language and a new way of life.

I miss Allie terribly, but I miss Mom and Dad more. I even miss the aggravation of dealing with six older brothers and living in a pink and white bedroom. But I'm healthy and I'm free ... and I'm learning to be happy.

But best of all, I'm hunting demons! Greg fights beside me as Wick once did, and together we're making the world a safer place for all of mankind.

COPYRIGHT

HER HIGHLAND YULE

1

———

*L*ady Catriona Logan swept into the great hall of Lastalrig Castle, her tartan skirt swishing around her ankles and her corsage laced so tightly she could feel her every breath. Hands fisted on hips, she paused to admire the decorations. The huge stone hearth at the far end of the room was swept clean, ready for the lighting of the Yule log when the men returned from procuring the traditional birch tree. The brass candle sconces fairly shone, having been polished for the festivities. Once the wicks were lit, the beeswax candles would cast a pearly glow on the rough stone walls. Fresh rushes were strewn across the flagstone floor, and the tables and walls were bedecked with holly, ivy, and mistletoe. In pride of place hung a beautifully woven kissing branch. The large spherical ornament was suspended from the rafters above a spot right in front of the head table where Cat and her highland laird Eideard would be seated.

Christmas at Lastalrig was like nothing Cat had ever experienced.

In the six months since she'd fallen through time to land in Eideard's life, she'd grown accustomed to the Scotland of 1452, but Christmas ... well, Christmas was a time for family and friends, for beloved traditions like twinkling lights on a decorated tree, caroling in the snow, and lazy Christmas mornings with hot chocolate, cinnamon rolls, and beautifully wrapped presents under the tree.

At least, that was what every other Christmas of her life had been. But this wasn't 2012 and she wasn't in North Carolina with Gran Da. No, this year she was the Lady of Lastalrig Castle in the year of our Lord fourteen hundred and fifty-two. And it wasn't even Christmas they'd be celebrating tonight. It was Yule, and the festivities would last twelve days, with the biggest celebration occurring on Twelfth Night, January 5th, the Eve of Epiphany.

Eideard had explained it all to her, making sure she understood her role for the various saints' days that fell between Christmas and Epiphany, and she was somewhat familiar from her university studies of medieval literature, but reading about something that happened hundreds of years ago and experiencing it first hand were vastly different beasts. At least she knew she could rely on Eideard to guide her through the intricacies of the season.

Eideard. Her highland laird. The love of her life and the reason she was here, in a castle that was little more than a moldering ruin in the time she'd been born to. Eideard. He'd loved her enough to discover a way for her to choose her fate, and once she'd recognized his forbearance as love, she'd followed her heart and chosen to stay.

She smiled, remembering his declaration of love, "Ye are a trial, Catriona. How could ye doubt my love? Have I nae forborne tae beat ye when all my kinsmen hae counseled me that ye needed naught but a good lashing tae learn your place?"

A giggle escaped her lips and she glanced around to be sure she was still alone. She'd actually had to explain to the poor man that not beating her didn't equal love in a 21st century woman's mind!

But regardless of their vastly different communication styles, not to mention world views, Eideard did love Catriona, and Cat loved him so deeply, so completely, that she'd given up the opportunity to return to her own time, and instead worked daily to settle into her new life as the laird's wife, the Lady of Lastalrig.

And even though it was Yule, not Christmas, and gifts would not be exchanged for centuries yet to come, Cat would hold to her own traditions. Her hands relaxed from their fists and slid across the folds of her tartan skirt to rest protectively over the slight swell of her belly. Tonight, in the seclusion of their bedchamber, she would give Eideard the most precious gift she'd ever held: the knowledge that she carried his child.

2

A few hours later, Cat sat beside Eideard at the high table enjoying a meal of roast goose and mince pies. The Yule log crackled merrily on the hearth providing both warmth and a rosy glow to the crowded room. Many of the members of Clan Logan had come to Lastalrig for the Yule celebration, and the castle teemed with life. Every room, except the bedchamber Cat shared with Eideard, boasted extra inhabitants, and the kitchens scurried to keep everyone fed.

Cat glanced at Eideard and her heart did a familiar little flip, raising her pulse. Her husband was easily the most handsome man in the room. Powerfully built with broad shoulders and a narrow waist, his dark auburn hair glistened in the firelight. He'd clubbed it at the back of his neck for the night's festivities, though Cat loved it best when it hung loose around his shoulders. As though feeling her gaze upon him, Eideard turned his head and smiled, his hazel eyes sparkling.

"Are ye enjoying the meal, love?" he asked, his English lilting with the Scots brogue she loved.

She nodded, heat suffusing her cheeks as she thought of

how his accent thickened when they made love in the private paradise of their marriage bed.

He grinned, and grabbing her hand, lifted it to his lips. "Ye are especially lovely tonight, Catriona. That new gown suits ye."

"Thank you, Eideard," she said, lowering her eyes demurely. "I'm glad my appearance pleases you."

Eideard chuckled, squeezed her hand, and, leaning close, whispered for her ear alone, "That was well said, my love. Ye'll have the clan believing ye are a well-bred lass yet." He kissed her cheek before continuing, "but 'tis a lucky man who knows the truth of who and what ye are ... and that man is me."

Heat rose throughout her body, and she knew that her cheeks flamed to match the red of her new gown. She widened her eyes, met his gaze more boldly than any fifteenth century woman would dream of, and said with a very good imitation of innocence, "Why, my lord, I cannot imagine what you mean. I can assure you, my breeding is excellent."

Eideard guffawed. When his mirth had settled, he raised his goblet to her. "To yer health, wife."

Cat lifted her own cup and said with a smile, "And to yours as well, husband," and took a sip. Alone of all the revelers in the great hall, Catriona drank water. Boiled water. Though the castle's supply of drinking water came from a pristine spring, Cat had given Mistress Mac, the castle's headwoman, instructions that any water she and Eideard consumed was to be boiled first. As soon as she suspected her pregnancy, Cat had stopped drinking the ale that was served with every meal and insisted on water. Mistress Mac might think her strange, but the headwoman had long since accepted that the laird's wife held some distinctly odd notions.

After the remains of the meal had been whisked away to the kitchens, several of the clansmen pushed the large trestle tables away from the center of the room, clearing a wide area before the high table.

"What's happening, Eideard?" Cat asked, leaning close to her husband.

Eideard's eyes widened and his brows lifted in surprise. "Did ye no tell me that folk still carol in yer time?" he asked in a whisper.

"Well, yes," she said, watching in fascination as several pipers prepared their bagpipes, "but everyone could just as easily sit at table and sing. Why is so much open space needed?"

"Sit at table and sing? I can see we've verra different ideas of caroling," he said with a wry smile. "Watch and learn, wife. Clan Logan will show you what it is to carol."

With that, Eideard rose from the table and clapped his hands. The room quieted except for the residual hum of a pipe as it continued to bleed air. The laird left the table and strode to the center of the cleared space.

"As Laird o' Lastalrig, I claim the first carol. Who will join me?"

Cat watched in wonder as men and women rushed to the open area and formed a large circle around their laird. Those who didn't join the circle climbed onto the tables at the edges of the room and settled to watch. When all were in place, Eideard nodded to the pipers and began to sing in a rich baritone. The bagpipes caught his melody and the folk in the circle moved to the intricate rhythms of the carol.

The song was like nothing Cat had ever experienced. Eideard sang in Scots Gaelic, and while her grasp of the language had vastly improved over the last six months, she had trouble following the words, buried as they were in unexpected rhythms, the shuffle of dancing feet, and the screel of bagpipes. Cat sighed. If she'd expected to find comfort in the familiarity of *traditional* Christmas carols, she would obviously be sorely disappointed. Instead, she straightened in her seat and chose to enjoy the spectacle. Gran Da would never believe this!

When his carol finished, Eideard bowed to the dancers and left the circle. Another singer took his place, a woman this time, and for a few moments the circle blurred as some left to sit on the tables and others took their places. Then, at a nod from the singer, the next carol began.

Eideard made his way back to Cat's side, dropped into his chair and drank deeply from his goblet. Wiping his mouth on his sleeve, he nodded to the circle. "That is how we carol at Lastalrig."

Cat smiled. "In my time, people walk about their neighborhoods in groups of five or six and sing Christmas carols. Or, if you're having a holiday party, everyone might sit around after dinner and sing. I've never seen carols accompanied by bagpipes and a circle dance."

Eideard shook his head, a small frown creasing his brow. "Everyone sings? How would they all agree on the melody?"

His words stunned her. "Agree on the melody? You mean it isn't standardized?"

He puzzled over her question for a moment before answering. "Standardized? Do ye mean everyone knows the carol? It doesna change with the singer?"

"That's right," she said with a nod. "The words and music are written down so everyone sings the carol the same way."

He stared at her. "How verra strange. Is it no boring to know exactly how it will sound?"

"Well, no. It's very comforting. You can relax into the music and remember other times, other places." Her eyes suddenly filled with tears as longing for her family and friends overwhelmed her.

Eideared picked up her hand and lifted it to his lips. "Dinna cry, lassie," he murmured. "Ye've home and family here now, and I'm verra glad ye chose to stay with me."

She wiped her eyes with her other hand and smiled at him. "So am I, my love." She drew a shuddering breath and turned to watch the carolers. "But it is so very different here."

When the next carol ended, Donal, Eideard's cousin and second in command, moved to stand before the high table. "Will the Lady o' Lastalrig not honor us wi' a carol?"

Cat's heart thundered so loudly that she almost missed Eideard's response when he rose to address the room. "My lady's customs are different," he said, his voice smooth as silk. "She is no accustomed to the dancing and the pipes."

She rose to stand beside him, squeezed his hand and said, "I'll gladly share one of my carols, and you're welcome to dance if you wish," she turned to the pipers and bowed her head, "but if you wouldn't mind, I'd ask you not to play."

The lead piper removed the blowstick from his mouth, bowed to her, and said, "We would be honored to listen to yer song, Lady."

Cat's thoughts raced. Which carol should she choose? Which would these people find most familiar? Which would make her seem least alien?

Eideard released her hand and seated himself beside her. The clan moved quietly out of the circle of dancers, waiting for her to begin.

When she sang the first note, the hall stilled. She hadn't realized she'd chosen until the words and melody emerged.

"Silent Night."

Her heart had chosen for her, and the choice was perfect. She sang the simple melody with all the warmth and longing in her soul. She sang for Gran Da and all the friends she would never see again. She sang for Eideard and the child growing within; for the future and the family they would build. She sang for Lastalrig Castle and the clan that had welcomed her, despite her odd ways. She sang for herself, for the woman she had been, and the one she was becoming.

When the last note faded away, Cat came to herself, suddenly embarrassed by the many eyes watching her. Then Donal began to clap and the hall filled with applause.

Eideard rose, pulled her into his arms, and whispered, "That was verra well done, Catriona. My people ... *your* people were moved."

When the hall quieted again, Donal bowed to her and said, "Thank you for sharing a carol, mi'lady." He turned to the hall and beckoned the people to gather. "Form a circle," he cried. "My own carol is burstin' to be sung!" And the hall filled again with what Cat was coming to recognize as Gaelic gaiety.

3

The party, or *ceilidh* as Eideard called it, was still going strong a few hours later. The music had become more boisterous and the dancing more frenetic, but the energy in the hall remained cheerful and full of good spirits. Unfortunately, Cat's energy was flagging.

Though her pregnancy was still in the early stages, she tired more easily and found herself seeking solitude more frequently. Peace and quiet restored her soul, and this evening's feast and festivities had been anything but tranquil.

She turned away from Eideard and tried to stifle a yawn, but her husband was too aware of her to be fooled.

"Are ye tired, lass? Do ye wish to retire?"

She smiled wearily. "I'm fine," she said, another yawn spoiling her attempt to deflect his concern. "I don't want to spoil your fun. You stay. I can see myself to our chamber."

"Nay, my love. We'll go together. None in this hall would knowingly cause ye harm, but some men are too far in their cups to notice who ye are." He stood and offered her his hand. "Come."

She took his hand and stood, appreciating his steady

strength as fatigue weighted her limbs. Together they left the hall, stopping here and there along the way to wish the joy of the season on various members of the clan.

When they reached their bedchamber, Cat sank into a chair before the hearth, blessing Mistress Mac for her foresight in seeing that the fire burned brightly.

Eideard knelt beside her chair and gazed earnestly into her eyes. "Are ye well, Catriona?" he asked, surprising her with his question.

"Of course," she said. "I'm just tired. It's been a long day."

He nodded, but his eyes continued to search her face. "Aye, it has, but ye seem to tire more easily these days. If there's aught amiss, ye'd tell me, would ye not?"

Her heart did a little backflip and she knew the moment had come. How she loved this man! She was out of her time and often out of her element, but he believed her, accepted her though she was so often not what the world expected of a woman in this time and place, and loved her wholeheartedly. The fates had blessed her when they had brought her to Eideard.

She smiled, joy flooding her soul. "Nothing is wrong, Eideard. In fact, something is very, very right." She took his hand and guided it to rest on her abdomen, the folds of her new red gown soft beneath their fingers. "I'm carrying your child," she said very softly, her voice husky with emotion.

Eideard's eyes had followed the movement of their hands, but now his gaze jumped to lock on hers and his hand spasmed on her belly.

"Truly?" he whispered. When she nodded, he asked, "Are ye certain?"

She laughed. "Well, if I were at home, I'd run down to the pharmacy and buy a pregnancy test, but since I can't pee on a stick here ..." She stopped, seeing the bewilderment in his eyes. "Yes, Eideard," she said simply. "I'm sure."

He bounced to his feet, pulled her from the chair, and swung her into his arms. Holding her as easily as if she were a child, he spun in a circle before depositing her on the bed. "I'm to be a father!"

Landing beside her, he wrapped her in his arms and kissed her thoroughly. When they broke apart, he stroked her hair and asked, "When?"

"Uhm, given that I've never been pregnant before, I'm just guessing," she said, grinning at the impatient growl she both heard and felt. "But by my calculations, I think mid-July."

"Ye've made me verra happy, my love," he said, nuzzling her neck, "but ye are wearin' too many layers for me to properly appreciate the wonder o' the moment."

Later, as they lay spooned beneath the blankets, Eideard's hand splayed protectively across her belly, Cat spoke into the peaceful quiet. "You know, in my time, it's traditional to give presents at Christmas." She squirmed around in his arms until they were nose to nose. "I think this," she pressed his hand to her belly again, "is the best Christmas present either of us is ever likely to receive."

He kissed her tenderly, and then rested his forehead against hers. "I know 'tis one I'm no likely to forget."

She laughed and said, "I can't wait to meet this baby. I wonder if it will be a boy or a girl?"

He kissed her forehead lightly. "I dinna know, but whichever it is, I will love it until the day I die ... just as I will its mother."

Lady Catriona Logan sighed happily, all nostalgia over Christmases past lost in the wonder of her first Highland Yule.

ALSO BY DEB LOGAN

Children's Stories and Chapter Books:

Cinnamon Chou Files:

- THE CASE OF THE MISSING INARIAN
- THE CASE OF THE GLITTERING HOARD
- THE CASE OF THE RECREATIONAL THIEF
- THE CASE OF THE VANISHING PUPPY

Prentiss Twins Novels:

- THUNDERBIRD
- COYOTE
- WHITE BUFFALO (A KINDLE VELLA SERIAL!)
- THE TWELVE DAYS OF TRICKSTERS (A PRENTISS TWINS SHORT STORY)

"Read-to-Me" Stories:

- CHATTERMASTER
- DEIRDRE'S DRAGON
- THE FOX AND THE FLEAS
- MOM'S HELPER
- READ-TO-ME STORIES (COLLECTION)

Short Stories:

- ANGELIC VOICES
- LILAH'S GHOST

Young Adult Stories and Novels:

Dani Erickson Stories:

- DEMON DAZE
- SCHOOL DAZE
- FAMILY DAZE
- CHALLENGING DAZE
- DANGEROUS DAZE
- DANI'S DEMONS (COLLECTION)

Faery Chronicles:

- FAERY UNEXPECTED (NOVEL)
- FAERY BEAUTIFUL (SHORT STORY)
- FAERY UNPREDICTABLE (NOVELETTE)
- LEXIE'S CHOICE (SHORT STORY)
- OF DRAGONS AND CENTAURS (SHORT STORY)
- FAERY COLLECTIBLE (COLLECTION)

Faery Serial in Kindle Vella:

- CONFESSIONS OF A TEENAGE TREE SPRITE

Feyland Tie-Ins:

- EMMA: A FEYLAND DRYAD
- ON GUARD: A FEYLAND STORY

Seer Chronicles:

- TERRORS
- TO HAVE...AND TO HOLD
- SELKIES IN PARADISE

- THE JOURNAL
- PALADIN SHIELD

Siren Tales:

- SALT WATER
- SIREN SURF

Short Story Collections:

- GHOSTS AND GHOULIES
- MORE GHOSTS AND GHOULIES

Short Fiction:

- AMELIA FOX: SPY IN TRAINING
- BEAUTY OR BUTTERFACE?
- RUSH!
- THAT LAKE HOUSE SUMMER

"WDM Presents" Anthologies:

- 2016: A YEAR OF SHORT FICTION
- 2017: A YEAR OF SHORT FICTION
- TALES OF MYSTERY & MAYHEM
- WDM PRESENTS: SHORT FICTION FROM 2020

ABOUT DEB LOGAN

Deb Logan specializes in tales for the young – and the young at heart! Author of the popular Faery Chronicles series, Deb loves the unknown, whether it's the lure of space or earthbound mythology. She writes about demon hunters, thunderbirds, and everyday life on a space station for tweens, teens, and anyone who enjoys young adult fiction. Her work has been published in multiple volumes of *Fiction River*, as well as in *2017 Young Explorer's Adventure Guide*, *Feyland Tales*, and other popular anthologies.

Sign up for Deb's newsletter and receive a FREE story!

To learn more, visit Deb at:
debloganwrites.com
Or send her an email at:
debloganwrites@gmail.com

ALSO BY DEBBIE MUMFORD

Kristi Lundrigan Mysteries:

- DELECTABLE MOUNTAIN QUILTING (NOVEL)
- FOOL'S PUZZLE (SHORT STORY)
- WILDFIRE! (SHORT STORY)

Gus and Ghost Short Story Series:

- SEVENTH
- SEVENTH: FIRST FRUITS
- DEATH OF AN ALCHEMIST (UNCOLLECTED ANTHOLOGY)
- SEVENTH: THE SAMHAIN DILEMMA

Logans of Lastalrig Series:

- HER HIGHLAND LAIRD (NOVELLA)
- HER HIGHLAND YULE (SHORT STORY)

Red's Series:

- RED'S MAGICK (SHORT STORY COLLECTION)
- SEEING RED (SHORT STORY)

Signs of the Prophecy Novels:

- YOUNGEST
- SEEKER
- CHOSEN (COMING SOON!)

Sorcha's Children Series:

- Sorcha's Children (Omnibus Edition)
- Sorcha's Heart (Novella)
- Dragons' Choice (Novel)
- Dragons' Flight (Novel)
- Dragons' Desire (Novel)
- Dragons' Destiny (Novel)

Supernatural Yellowstone Short Story Series:

- Reality Bites
- The Cat Lady of Yellowstone

Uncollected Anthology Short Stories:

- Death of an Alchemist (UA Alchemy)
- The Wedding Cake (UA Magical Arts)

Universal Star League Short Story Series:

- The Warbirds of Absaroka
- Awakening the Warrior
- Incident on the Odyssey
- The Queen's Captive
- The Lost Colony
- Voyages Into The Black (Collection)

Witchling Short Story Series:

- Witchling
- The Solitary Sorceress
- To Protect a Princess

Stand Alone Novels:

- SECOND SIGHT

Short Story Collections:

- LOVE IN A FLASH
- TALES OF BYGONE DAYS
- TALES OF LOVE & MAGICK
- TALES OF THE UNEXPECTED
- TALES OF TOMORROW
- TALES OF DISASTROUS DEEDS

Short Fiction:

- A WALK WITH GEORGIA
- ASTROMANCER
- BENEATH AND BEYOND
- DEEP DREAMING
- DELIA'S DECISION
- ICE STORM
- INCIDENT ON THE HIGH LINE
- MISS BAINBRIDGE'S SUMMER ADVENTURE
- NEEDLE-GREEN
- NEW YEAR
- OPENING HER EYES
- REMEMBRANCE
- SILVER-TIPPED DEATH
- SISTERS IN SUFFRAGE
- SKYE DREAMS
- SPINNING
- THE TIE THAT BINDS
- THE TRAIL WHERE WE CRIED

- THE WHITE DRAGON AND THE RED
- TO DREAM OF FLYING
- TREASURES
- WAKINYAN'S VALLEY

"WDM Presents" Anthologies:

- 2016: A YEAR OF SHORT FICTION
- 2017: A YEAR OF SHORT FICTION
- TALES OF MYSTERY & MAYHEM
- WDM PRESENTS: SHORT FICTION FROM 2020

ABOUT DEBBIE MUMFORD

Debbie Mumford specializes in speculative fiction (fantasy, paranormal romance, and science fiction) as well as mystery and historical fiction. Author of the popular *Sorcha's Children* series, Debbie loves the unknown, whether it's the lure of space or earthbound mythology. Her work has been published in multiple volumes of *Fiction River*, as well as in *Heart's Kiss Magazine*, *Amazing Monster Tales*, and many other popular anthologies. She writes about dragon-shifters, time-traveling lovers, and detectives—whether amateur or professional.

Join Debbie's special announcement newsletter list and receive a FREE story!

To learn more, visit Debbie at:
debbiemumford.com/
Or send her an email at:
deborah.mumford@gmail.com

facebook.com/DebbieMumfordWrites

amazon.com/author/debbiemumford

bookbub.com/authors/debbie-mumford

twitter.com/deborah_mumford